Meant to Be

JEA HAWKINS

Wicked Hearts Publishing

PUBLISHED BY WICKED HEARTS PUBLISHING

COPYRIGHT 2016 BY JEA HAWKINS

COVER ART BY SATYR DESIGNS

FIRST EDITION
ISBN-13: 978-1546935889

Chapter 1

"Turn it off," Alice commanded, her gaze still focused on the papers on the table. She had promised her client a completed file by the end of the week and time was running out. Normally, she would work in her office, but she wanted to spread the papers out and get them better organized.

Although she tried to concentrate on what she was doing, the music blaring from the TV and the even louder announcer's voice made it impossible. Why did teenagers have to have the volume so loud?

"I told you to turn it off." Her voice rose above the music. Alice hated yelling at anyone, especially her daughter, but it felt like Liza had a special kind of torture in mind for her today. She supposed her daughter was excited to be on winter break.

"But it's Misty Morse!" Liza trilled. "She's incredible!" To Alice's chagrin, her daughter was actually dancing to the music, her hips swaying in a way she thought was far too salacious for a sixteen-year-old. And she would forbid it if not for the fact that she, too, had once danced like that. Twenty years ago…

"I don't care if it's that Bieber kid all the girls love. Turn it off," she said again, her voice firmer. "And you look ridiculous, like your hips are going to fall off any minute. Misty isn't Beyoncé, doofus."

"Mom, do you even know who Beyoncé is?"

"She says girls rule the world, but apparently moms don't in this house." After another moment passed, Alice pressed her hand to her forehead. "Elizabeth Jane Cavanaugh, I swear if you don't turn it off, I will change every vowel in your name to y. Don't make me inflict that kind of pain on you."

Her daughter's sharp, loud intake of breath let her know she was finally listening. "You wouldn't dare do something like that. That's just evil."

"I've been your mother since you were born. You know no one is more evil than I am, and I would do it, so you can fit in with all the Madysyns of the world. I will make your life a complete nightmare. Now turn it off."

"Mom." Liza turned off the television and walked up to the kitchen table, her hips still moving a little too emphatically. As much as Alice tried to remind herself

Liza was growing up and there was no stopping the process, it wasn't something she liked to dwell on.

How had the years gone by so quickly? Sure, Alice was thirty-eight now, but she still felt like a kid herself sometimes. So the idea of her daughter outpacing her in adulthood? Not fair.

Liza pressed her palms against the table's surface and glared at her, her green eyes narrowed. "Remember you went to school with Misty forever ago?"

"Of course I remember. The nineties weren't forever ago, child. What's your point?" Alice snapped, leaning back in her chair and folding her arms. Leave it to Liza to bring up something Alice didn't want to discuss. It was her adolescent super power.

"My point is if you don't remember, then allow me to pull out the Class of '96 yearbook that has a whole bunch of pictures of you two together. I hear from Aunt Kathy you and Misty were inseparable – doing your homework together, hanging out while she played guitar in the garage. You always say you remember what it was like to be my age, so don't you remember all the fun you had with her back then and can't you let me have fun listening to her music now?"

With a sigh, Alice relaxed her hands on either side of the paperwork, looked up at her daughter with eyes that were just as green as hers, and said in a low voice, "Of course I remember, Liza, and I want you to enjoy whatever you want to listen to. But as far as that friendship, things change. Misty made a choice to leave this town a long time ago and I made a choice to stay here, and then I got to have you. It's been twenty years since graduation. Our lives took different paths and if you don't mind, I would really like to get this done so I can finish this pedigree chart, all right?"

"Fine." Liza leaned over and whispered, "But are you going to be this calm, cool, and collected when she comes to town next week for the reunion and to give a New Year's concert at the high school? I think not. I think you're going to remember what a fantastic time you had being a teenager with her and loosen up."

"Hey, I am plenty loose, as evidenced by your existence." Alice jabbed her finger in Liza's direction.

"Fine. So what happened to you between my birth and now?" Liza challenged.

Rolling her eyes, Alice decided the safest place to look was at the file she was trying to complete.

"Mom, are you going to answer my questions?"

"Um, no. A mother's looseness is not for a daughter to question or comprehend."

"Juicy secrets, eh? Small town soap opera where once best friends are now on the outs? Of all the times you told me about your childhood, you never talked about Misty to me. I had to find out from around town about what good friends you were. Why haven't you ever told me about her? It's not like she's some nobody. She's a celebrity and she was your best friend once upon a time."

Alice blew out a breath. Leave it to Liza to dig up things she didn't want to recall. "There's nothing to tell. Ancient history." Deflecting. Sure. That would work.

"People only call something 'ancient history' when there's a relationship involved." Liza narrowed her eyes. "Were you two a thing?"

"Are you my father?" Alice finally asked, throwing her hands in the air. "Because, seriously, that's who you sound like right now."

"Well, I was wondering if that's why no one else has ever lasted in your life – if maybe Misty the superstar is also the girl who got away." Liza sank into a chair at the table and rested her face on the palm of her hand, mirroring one of her mother's favorite poses. "Fess up, Mom. I've seen you go on less than a dozen dates with a handful of women in the past sixteen years and none of them got beyond the second date."

Covering her face with her hands, Alice leaned against the table. "I'd love to know what inspired this interrogation, but I choose waterboarding, if that's an option."

"Mom, please. We already had the 'mommy-likes-women' talk ages ago when I asked why I don't have a father. Why can't we talk about this now?"

"Because I'm not ready to talk about Misty now, if ever, let alone see her." Alice finally lifted her face to look into Liza's eyes.

She knew she was fortunate to have an intelligent, tough, confident daughter. What drove her nuts was how damn perceptive Liza was in addition to all of that. Liza was a lot like the Misty that Alice had once known –

creative and able to see beyond appearances. But she also took after her own mother, tenacious and a little too nosy. Sometimes Alice had to redirect Liza's analytical tendencies, just to keep her own sanity.

"You know, you'd make an excellent genealogist," she told Liza. "Are you sure you want to study music? Seriously, the Archives could use a researcher like you."

"Wow, so it's that bad?" Liza was still staring at her, chin resting in her hand. The girl was impossible.

Alice nodded. This was a battle she had better concede before it turned into full blown warfare. "It's that bad."

"Like… pizza, beer, and bad B-movie night bad?"

"Worse."

"Ouch." Liza's brow furrowed.

"I know. Look, tell you what – I promise I'll explain everything, but I can't do it under this kind of pressure."

Looking at her sideways, Liza pursed her lips and said, "Fine. You owe me. How about you tell me all about it during our annual Christmas Eve movie marathon."

"That's…" Alice glanced at the calendar hanging on

the refrigerator. Today was already December 21. "So soon."

"Well, it's that or I keep pestering you." Liza rose from the table. "The fact is Misty Morse is a huge star and I want to be a music producer, so I have every intention of meeting her when she's in town this week. Plus, she'll be at your high school reunion and the whole town is going to be at her concert. Where will you be?"

Alice looked up and stared open-mouthed after her daughter as she sauntered away, her long dark brown hair swaying against her back. "Shit," she muttered when Liza was gone. After another moment, she ran her hands through her own dark waves, and then reached for her cell phone and selected a number in the contact list.

Deb answered after only one ring. "Hey, what's up, lady?"

"Did you know Misty Morse is coming home for our twentieth year class reunion and then putting on some kind of concert?"

"Of course I did. Everyone in four towns knows about that. Didn't you?"

"No." Alice looked at the papers fanned out on the

table between her elbows. "That's a lie. I mean, I sort of knew, but I've been working and trying to ignore the fact that the reunion is looming."

"You're always working. If you're not at the Archives, you're working on research for clients. Do you ever have fun?"

"I love what I do. It is fun." Even though Alice tried not to sound petulant, she couldn't keep the whine out of her voice.

Deb released an exasperated sigh. "I suppose you're working extra hours so you can avoid the whole Misty thing and have an excuse to only 'sort of' know about it. You always did like to pretend stupidity to get out of things. Not that I begrudge you that – you make it work, somehow."

Alice's nostrils flared a bit. "No, I'm looking for an excuse to avoid the whole being twenty years older thing. How am I thirty-eight? Thirty-eight, Deb. We've been out of high school for twenty years. Besides, someone has to keep a roof over my daughter's head so she can dance around like an idiot to music that is definitely not Nirvana or R.E.M."

"Teenagers, yeesh. What a pain in the ass she must be, being all modern and shit."

"You don't know the half of it. Well, I guess you do, since you put up with her kind every day. So, I suppose I should find out what's up with Misty coming back to town, right?"

"Yeah, you probably should. It'll make avoiding her that much easier. So, yeah, Misty is coming to our class reunion and she's giving a free concert at the high school on New Year's Eve, too. I suppose it's meant to be a big promotional thing. The local media is calling it 'Misty Morse: The Homecoming' or something like that. It's probably a golden marketing opportunity for her, you know? The kids are flipping their shit." Sometimes it was hard to believe Deb was a teacher, considering the way she spoke, but Alice knew her flippant attitude was what made her so popular with the high school students. Deb was the "cool" teacher.

With a grimace, Alice glanced back up at the darkened television. "Please tell me there's something else we can do on New Year's Eve, then." Her voice came out drier than she expected.

"There's always something else to do. I have to work the concert since it's a school event, but you can go into Montpelier, if you want, and get far away from the whole thing. Is your daughter going to the concert?"

"Oh yeah, I'm sure she'll camp out there if that's what it takes to meet Misty." She licked her lips and tried to focus on the papers in front of her, but the words no longer made sense.

It was Wednesday afternoon. The reunion was on Friday night and New Year's Eve was just over a week later. How could she have managed to tune out all the details, even willfully? Sure, there was quite a bit she'd tried to tune out this year, but this? This was, for all intents and purposes, like an ex coming home and that was a big deal. And maybe if she was a proper ex, she would have been internet-stalking Misty's every move for the past twenty years.

But the thing was she wasn't *exactly* an ex in the romantic sense. She was a could-have-been who had the sense to let go of a crush that had no future.

"And then there's the reunion," she muttered, almost forgetting she had her phone in her hand. "What am I going to do about that?"

Deb's voice drew her from her thoughts. "Come on, this is Misty. We've cheered her on since high school. I know what happened between you still hurts, but you should go to the reunion and see her, and you really should be at the concert to support her."

With a roll of her eyes, Alice looked at the calendar hanging on the kitchen wall. "Fine, I'll still go to the reunion as long as you don't leave me hanging. What time is the concert?"

"The actual show starts at ten."

"That's kind of late."

"Well, I think they're planning on an hour of music and then some food and a New Year's countdown. Why don't you ask Liza what her plans are for it?"

"I'm sure she'll be there with her friends, acting like a typical sixteen-year-old." Alice huffed into the phone. "I'll get the info as long as you don't make me go alone."

"Now you're the one sounding like a child. I already told you, I have to be at the school to help with set-up, but it shouldn't be difficult for you to find a date, if you don't mind going hetero for the night."

"Ugh. No thanks. You saw what the last hetero date got me."

"Ah yes, you caught the motherhood from that one."

Deb's voice sounded far away for a moment. "Sorry, but I've got to go. We'll do Whammy Bar tomorrow night and talk some more, all right?"

Alice nodded until she heard Deb say her name.

"Sorry. Yes. I'm nodding. See you tomorrow night."

When she set the cell back down on the table, she leaned over and pressed her forehead against the paperwork.

How long had she crushed on her best friend, Misty? And how long had she waited at her side, hoping the wannabe rock star would follow through on their adolescent plans to go on an adventure together, in search of fame, fortune, and more?

But it had never happened. No wild road trip together. No seeing the country. No picking up and moving to Seattle, like they had spent two years discussing. Just that bombshell decision one night that Misty was leaving right after graduation in hopes of making it big. Alone.

After that, there was no keeping up with Misty. Every "You've Got Mail" announcement back then had made Alice's heart leap. It seemed like there was one every day in 1996 and well into 1997. Emails that said things like, "Holy crap, standing where Kurt Cobain played his first gig ever!!!"

Until Misty got her manager, her first recording contract with a major label, played at Lilith Fair...

And then, no more emails. No more, "I'm going to fly you out here to be a part of all of this."

Nor did they ever discuss their prom, when Misty declared that the only person for her was Alice, and they decided to go stag so they could dance together.

Or that graduation night when they had shared a bittersweet kiss that could have been so much more, if Misty hadn't held back and then announced the change of plans – that she was leaving for Seattle without Alice.

Where had they gone wrong? How had their paths diverged to the point where they had stopped communicating, Alice had gotten knocked up, and Misty had become a star?

Alice gathered her paperwork with another huff of

frustration. Her gaze landed on a blue hardcover book sitting on the coffee table. "Damn it, Liza," she grumbled, setting her paperwork back down on the table and stalking into the living room. She bent and scooped the book up in her hand, hesitating as she did.

Their high school served several small communities in Vermont around Montpelier and it was a close-knit school. At least, it had been when she attended. She didn't know if things had changed since then, but Liza seemed happy enough with her classmates and teachers.

Sinking down onto the couch, Alice opened the 1996 yearbook and looked at the handwriting that covered all the white space on the inside cover's endpaper. Misty's scrawled note had made her laugh until she cried. No one in their class had been more popular than Misty Morse, she of the infinite amounts of cool. Misty certainly had not been voted "Most Likely to Succeed" or chosen as valedictorian – that had been Alice – but she was talented and well-liked.

Alice flipped through the oversized pages of the book. There certainly were many photographs of the two of them together, as well as Alice leaning over the school library circulation desk as she assisted a student. And then there was Misty on the stage in the auditorium, singing during the annual talent show.

They had followed the paths they both set for themselves – Misty becoming a singer and Alice going to college to pursue her degree in information and library science. Of course, pregnancy hadn't been in the plans, but she loved being a mother.

Sitting back on the couch, Alice drew her fingers down over one of the pages. This was her favorite photo – Misty and Alice slow-dancing together at the prom. She didn't know how they'd managed to take that picture, let alone squeeze it into the yearbook under deadline, but there it was. Under it, another friend had written "Hail to the Prom Queen and Queen!" Of course, neither of them was voted Prom Queen, let alone queens together, but it had been fun to have the students refer to them that way until after graduation, when everyone went their separate ways.

On the endpaper inside the back cover was another note from Misty, this one in large block letters with doodles around it: "Best Friends Forever."

Alice let the book close in her hand and let out a breath.

Why had forever ended only a year later?

And why did she feel like her love for Misty had never changed?

Chapter 2

"Just don't make me have to drive to that little pissant town you came from and drag you back here, got it?" Rick's voice pinged through the cell phone Misty held pressed to her ear. She hardly paid attention, though, as she craned her head to watch the scenery pass outside the window of the limousine. "Are you listening to me? We've got a deadline and I can't believe you would just run off like this without telling me until the last minute."

Misty drummed her fingers against her denim-clad legs and tried to ignore the leaping of her heart every time the car drove past a familiar sight. "Don't be like that," she said. "First of all, there's nothing wrong with Calais."

"Honey, everything is wrong with Calais. I mean, seriously, where should I start?" She could imagine Rick lowering his eyelashes and shaking his head with its bleach-blond hair. "Still, I suppose New England does grow them cool. Just look at Phish."

"Dude, only one of them is from New England. The rest are from other parts of the U.S.," Misty pointed out.

"They just happened to meet at the University of Vermont." She gathered her long, dark ponytail in her hand and gave her smooth, straight hair a tug before letting it go. For a manager, Rick could be very un-hip to the music industry.

"Oh. Right." Rick let out a long, wavering sigh. Misty tried not to laugh at him. Rick had a one-track mind and that track was paved with dollar bills. Being his biggest client wasn't all it was cracked up to be, but Misty knew Rick's tenacity and devotion was a huge factor in her success over the past twenty years.

Twenty years. Damn. Misty looked out at the rolling fields covered with a fresh, light layer of snow that made her think of powdered sugar. Her manager was a bit dramatic, but he was good for business. It probably didn't hurt that she had been his first client all those years ago. They had a bond – two people from small towns chasing their dreams. Two *gay* people. Rick liked to joke that he was the sister Misty never had and she tried not to snort with laughter when he did.

But he was no substitute for Alice.

Alice, the best friend Misty had less and less time for

when she hit it big, and then who ended up pregnant. At that point, Misty hadn't wanted to bother her. She knew children were a huge responsibility. She also didn't understand how Alice had ended up pregnant, considering she'd never had a boyfriend, let alone a date.

Rather than work through that head-scratcher, Misty had let it go. The music industry was a shark tank and, for the past twenty years, she had been in the middle of one hell of a feeding frenzy. Everyone wanted her – managers, agents, record labels, fans – it was never ending. Misty wanted only one thing, though, and that was to kick back and relax with the people she knew and trusted.

And reconnect with the woman she had been stupid enough to walk away from so long ago.

It was cheesy, sure, but she missed the group the townsfolk had dubbed "The Whammy Bar Kids." She wondered what it would be like to see them again – the loudmouthed twins, Deb and Derek, Nick with all his goofy jokes, and Alice. Beautiful, dependable, high-strung Alice with her quick wit and sharp retorts to everything anyone said.

She shifted in the seat of the car as she remembered her best friend's intense green eyes and long, dark, wavy hair. Alice, the loyal one who knew what she wanted and how to get it. During their high school years, they had talked about her going with Misty and working at a hip book store in Seattle, while Misty tried to make a name for herself playing gigs in coffeehouses and bars.

Unfortunately, Alice was also a huge distraction. Not a day went by that Misty didn't want to find a way to make Alice's witty, logical façade waver. In high school, no one could tempt her with alcohol, cigarettes, or even sex. Everyone had tried. Everyone but Misty until the one night she was ready to make the leap, only to realize she had exposed every one of Alice's vulnerabilities by telling her she planned to leave without her.

Because Misty knew if she started, she'd never want to stop. She also knew Alice would be better off waiting until Misty had gotten settled. After all, Seattle was across the country. Where would they live? What if they didn't find jobs right away? What about–

"Yo. Earth to Misty," Rick snapped into the phone.

"Sorry," she said, even though she wasn't. Why had

she made these plans without telling Rick until the moment her car arrived to bring her to the airport? Because Rick was, well, Rick.

And he was pressuring her to sign a new contract with her label before the end of the year, something she wasn't ready to contemplate just yet.

"Are you nearly there? Home sweet hovel?"

Misty returned her attention to the scenery and realized they had stopped in front of her father's house. She let out a breath and opened the door before the chauffeur could do it. As she rose from the car, she gripped the top of the door to steady herself.

"What if everyone thinks I'm some kind of asshole," she muttered to no one in particular.

Before her worry could grow and cycle out of control, Rick said loudly, "So you're there?"

"Yeah, sorry, I'm here."

"Fine. Check your email for that new contract, print it, sign it, and FedEx it back to me. I take it you've got FedEx out there in the sticks?"

"I don't know. It could be tricky, what with that dial-up internet and all." As much as Rick despised his small town roots, Misty loved hers. It was one of the reasons she was excited to attend her high school reunion.

"Whatever," Rick said, his annoyance coming through loud and clear. "Just do it and make sure you take my calls. I need to keep you accountable, understand?"

Misty blew out a breath and propped her free hand on her hip. "Meaning what?"

"Meaning I can't have you getting all nostalgic about your home planet, and then decide never to come back."

That hit far too close to home for Misty. She was well aware her current recording contract with the label expired in only nine days and she hadn't signed the new one Rick presented to her before they left L.A. She thrust her hand into her back pocket, hoping she sounded more relaxed than she felt. On the inside, though, her heart was pounding so hard, she thought she might pass out. This trip meant so much more to her than just a chance to see her father, go to the reunion, and give a small concert. She had to make a major decision about her career. Soon.

"My dad is waiting. I need to go."

"Fine. Text me as soon as you get that contract into the hands of the FedEx people, got that?"

"Yeah, I got it." Misty ended the call before Rick could say anything else about the contract or her visit home. It was like he didn't think she was entitled to some time off, some freedom to do her own thing.

And that was exactly why the last thing she wanted to do was sign that contract.

Misty turned and trotted up the steps to the front porch. Dad hadn't changed a thing while she was living her life across the country. As with her previous visits home, it didn't look like her dad even bothered to use the money she had sent back home over the years. The old screen door still creaked when she opened it. The top half of the weathered Dutch door was open, so she turned the knob and pushed the bottom half in as she called, "Dad?"

The house was the same on the inside, too, with faded wallpaper Misty remembered from her childhood and a spindly-legged telephone table in the front hall that had once belonged to one of her great-grandmothers. A warm sense of nostalgia filled her and she paused on the threshold to take a long, deep breath. She was home.

After a moment, she called "Dad?" again.

"There you are." A door from somewhere in the house slammed and footsteps approached.

Misty grinned as the man entered the front hall from the kitchen. She got her looks from her dad. They were both tall with dark brown hair that had a reddish tinge to it in the right light, and hazel eyes that could go green or gold, depending on what they wore. Her dad's plain gray t-shirt stretched across his broad chest. When he opened his arms, Misty walked into them. Her father's tight hug was still strong and comforting.

"Why do you always have to wait so long between visits?" he asked.

"Come on, Dad." Misty ducked as her father reached over to tug on her ponytail. "Hey!"

"I know you're going to say it's about time, but I finally took that money you sent and used it to fix up the foundation and finish the basement. Wait until you see it." Mr. Morse turned from his daughter and extended his hand to the chauffeur, who stood behind Misty with her luggage. "You must be her driver. I'm happy to help."

"Thank you, sir, but I've got this, if you'll just direct me." The driver was from a company Rick always used when they came to New England. Misty had booked the service behind Rick's back, of course, and asked for a more modest car since she hated limos.

"Upstairs, turn to the right, and it's the first door on the right," she told the driver. "And thanks."

"Why don't you get yourself a soda?" her father asked as the driver walked upstairs. "Get him one too, for the road."

"Sounds good." Misty turned away and went to the refrigerator to check the stash. Sure enough, her father had filled one shelf with plenty of Misty's favorite root beer. She reached in and plucked out one of the old-fashioned glass bottles. Twisting off the cap, she tossed it in the nearby trash can and lifted the bottle to her lips. It was a local brand of soda Misty couldn't find west or south of New England. That prickle of bubbles on her tongue and the sassafras-sweet flavor welcomed her home.

"Come check this out, Misty." Her father waved for her to follow, so she picked up a second bottle and went to meet her father.

Nothing in the mid-1800s farmhouse had changed, as far as Misty could tell, but when she saw the basement stairs, her breath caught. Instead of rickety wooden planks on a diagonal frame, there was an actual staircase leading down. And the musty storage area with cement floor and walls was now divided into two areas. There was a family room with drywall over the original walls and carpet on the floor. Just beyond it, Misty noticed a small studio where the instruments and music she had collected throughout junior high and high school were stored.

"Dad, this looks great," she said. "Wow. I didn't expect this. It must have been a big job."

"It was, but thanks to your generosity, I hired someone to do it, rather than doing it myself. It's a really nice getaway for me." Jim put his hands on his hips and nodded as he looked around. "Been a great place for me and the guys to watch the games. No one can hear us hollering and there's plenty of room for everyone. And I thought maybe you could work down here when you visit again. The sounds don't bother anyone." He gestured to the two sofas flanked by cushy recliners. The coffee table between them and the large-screen TV looked like they could set out an entire Super Bowl snack spread on it.

"Nice, Dad." Misty crouched to look at the huge television. "You bought this too?"

"Yup and I still have plenty to spend. The next project is replacing the furnace and water heater. I figure I'll work my way up until the house is like new again. I don't know if you'll want it someday, but it's time this stuff was done."

Her father looked very proud and Misty felt her own heart swell with pride that she'd been able to help him make this happen. The house had been in their family since one of her distant great-grandfathers built it, but as a single father Jim didn't exactly have the time or money to keep it in good repair. Now it looked like he was making the most of his empty nest, and Misty was glad she could make such a significant contribution with her hard-earned fame and fortune.

"We should really give the driver a hand with the bags," her father said, and turned back to the staircase.

Misty followed him, gave the driver the bottle of soda, and a hefty tip. The only other item left to bring into the house was her guitar case, which she let her father carry, since he insisted. It felt good to get away from everything – as far away as possible from her manager, her label, and her crazy, but lonely lifestyle. As she turned and walked back up the stairs to follow her father, she took in a deep breath.

There really was no place like home for the holidays. Her father was right – she didn't visit often enough. Over the years, she'd only had a day or two here and there to see him.

Only, this time, she would stay for almost two long weeks with family and old friends. She would see everyone and catch up with them. And hope they wouldn't think she was some kind of pretentious superstar…

Misty's father left her guitar leaning against the wall in her old bedroom and said, "I'll be downstairs. I'm sure you want to take a little time to yourself after such a long flight."

"Thanks, Dad." Misty smiled and watched as he left.

She was glad to see that even in his early sixties, he was still in good health and active. She supposed the latter was probably one of the reasons for the former.

Misty turned to her bedroom, leaned against the doorframe, and looked inside. Like the outside of the house, nothing here had changed. The walls still had that gray striped wallpaper she had found bland as a child, but grew to love when she was a teenager. Black curtains still hung on her window and all her rock idol posters from the 80s and 90s were on the walls.

There had been no time for her to redecorate during her short, sporadic visits, and her father assured her the room could stay the way it was indefinitely. Misty finally strolled in and nudged her suitcase with her foot, then sat on her bed.

It dipped with her weight and she patted the black comforter dotted with a pattern of pale pink skulls and crossbones. There were a lot of memories here – memories of sleepovers with Alice, talking about their goals, the life they wanted to build together, giggling, dreaming, planning…

With an exhalation, Misty raised her head and looked

around the room. The last time they had been here was prom night, after the dance, undressing and talking about what they would do in three weeks after graduation.

Before Misty decided it wasn't the right path for her best friend.

Not just yet.

Alice deserved more. She was too smart to go gallivanting off across the country with Misty. She belonged in college, getting her education. Misty couldn't let her throw it all away on the off chance that Misty might get a big break. She couldn't allow Alice to risk it, when staying home with her parents would guarantee her that degree in library science.

Misty also couldn't forget their kiss the night of graduation.

A kiss full of hope and desire, and Alice's usual resolve.

And then tears after, when she told Alice no – that they wouldn't be leaving together. There was one bus ticket to Seattle. For Misty alone.

I was so damn stupid.

Tonight, however, she was going to have to face her

past. With the reunion tomorrow, she knew she had to find Alice and try to figure out how she was going to make up for her mistake twenty years ago. If the Whammy Bar Kids still kept their Thursday night tradition, then she knew where she would find Alice.

Misty had spent years imagining how things would go when she finally worked up the courage to confront Alice. Now she flopped back on the bed and stared up at the ceiling. She wondered if the glow-in-the-dark stickers of stars and planets she had stuck up there would still glow when she turned out the lights, her very own personal galaxy of constellations.

She also wondered if Alice would snark at her like a yappy dog. That was her way, after all. Get on her bad side and she would make you sorry. Despite that, Alice was adorable and every time she yapped, Misty had wanted to kiss her until she melted.

Of course, she had never told her that. Then again, she hadn't known until graduation night when Alice surprised her with the kiss that the feeling was mutual.

What a way to blow it.

Misty let her head loll against the mattress and

spread her arms to either side, taking a moment to put herself back into her teenaged self's shoes. What *should* she have done that night? Had she made the right decision? Did it matter anyway, since they couldn't go back in time and change anything?

The cuckoo clock downstairs went off, letting her know it was going on four o'clock. With a groan, she rolled over onto her stomach and looked out the window at the backyard. Even her old tire swing still hung from the immense oak tree.

Yes, she really was home.

And part of her didn't want to leave it ever again.

Chapter 3

"So, do you think she's turned into some kind of an asshole or something? I mean, why do you want to avoid her so badly?" Derek divvied up the pizza slices and slid the plates in front of Deb and Alice. It was, for all intents and purposes, their usual Thursday night routine – dinner at the Whammy Bar to celebrate the "almost-weekend," as Deb had dubbed it back in 1994.

At first, it had been their way to unwind before Friday during their sophomore year when SATs and other adult decisions loomed. As they got older, it was where they gathered during college breaks, since they all went to different universities in the northeast, and then it became a regular tradition again when they returned to their hometown and obtained jobs as productive members of society. No matter where they lived and worked, Thursday nights at the Whammy Bar were a time-honored tradition.

These days, Deb's excuse was that working with teenagers required regular decompression. Derek was a local journalist covering school sports, so going to the Whammy Bar was as exciting as his work week got. As

far as Alice was concerned, there was nothing to
decompress from – she loved her work at the Vermont
State Archives and her daughter was old enough to fend
for herself, for the most part.

"Is Misty all we're going to talk about tonight?" Deb
nudged her twin brother and shook her head, her short
blonde bob swinging with the movement. "It's bad
enough I have to hear about her every day at school and
Alice made it clear she doesn't want to get into this, so
we need to just drop it."

"But the reunion *is* tomorrow night, which means
she's going to be in town over Christmas and then for
her New Year's concert," Derek pointed out.

"Holy shit, we've discussed this ad nauseam. It's a
thing. It's happening. Let it go." Deb's hand curled over
Alice's arm, giving a squeeze. "Look, however you want
to handle this – whether you want to go or not, I'll
support that decision. It's our twentieth reunion and we
really shouldn't skip out on it, but I understand if you'd
rather not go."

Alice ducked her head and crammed the pizza into
her mouth, ignoring the fact the melted cheese had that

lava-like quality she hated. After yesterday, she had to accept that the news about Misty's concert was all the locals in Calais could talk about – heck, even people in Montpelier were gushing about it, as she realized during work today when she finally forced herself to pay attention to the world around her. Like a controversial topic that people on social media refused to drop, there was no tuning this out either.

Not that Alice hadn't tried – she wanted to at least be aware, but not inundated with Misty Morse this and that. So she had immersed herself in work all day. The books at the Vermont State Archives had never stood up straighter on the shelves, all nudged into place by Alice as she hid in the stacks. Unfortunately, even that hadn't protected her from hearing Misty's name over and over again throughout the day.

She caught Derek watching her and muttered, "What?" around a mouthful of pizza.

"I had no idea you would not be okay with this," he said, his voice filled with concern.

"It's a free country." Alice shrugged. "Pass the hot sauce, please."

"Yeah, it's a free country and all, but that's not the point." Deb handed the bottle of hot sauce across the table before her brother could get it. "Pay attention, Derek. We all know how much it hurt Alice when Misty left without her. We always thought she'd take her along. That's all we talked about in 1996 and then, well, it didn't happen."

Derek leaned back in his chair, looking crestfallen. Brow furrowed, he asked, "Did she ever write or call to explain why it never happened?"

Alice shook her head. "We kept in touch for about a year and the only thing she said was she wanted me to go to college. Then the emails slowed down while she got famous, and then I got pregnant, and…" Her shoulders rose in a shrug, lingering for a moment before falling. "That was that. But, like you said, it's a free country."

"I didn't say that – Deb did."

"Oh. Right." Alice shifted her weight and kept her eyes on the pizza. The fact that she felt like she was dying inside couldn't stand in the way of hanging out with the friends who *had* stuck with her through the years. "Can we talk about something else, like where the heck is Nick?"

Deb made a choking noise and waved at Alice. "Oh, wait, wait, this is such a good one, you're not even going to believe it. Are you ready?"

"Ready for what?" Alice raised her gaze to Deb's reddened face. Whatever her friend had to say, it must have been juicy, because Deb's skin only got ruddier by the moment.

Beside her, however, Alice felt Derek tense up and heard him whisper, "Oh, shit..." Following his gaze, she looked over the heads of the patrons at the tables at the bar and grill, at the front door and saw *her*.

The predictable world Alice had lived in for the past two decades turned upside down. Romance wasn't exactly in her nature. She was ruled by common sense and an inability to keep from blurting out the first thing that came to mind. It was, she knew, her defense mechanism – using humor to hide her feelings.

But in this moment, her life was ruled by the one who got away.

What do I do?

Even though she was sure she merely thought it, she must have spoken out loud, because Derek said, "I don't know." His eyes went wide and he wheezed, "She's coming this way. Holy crap, do you think she remembers us?"

Deb rolled her eyes. "Being famous doesn't wipe out your memories, dumbass. Just... be cool."

"When has Derek ever been cool?" Alice shifted her gaze to Deb, but it was drawn back to Misty who stood at the bar in her black leather jacket and blue jeans, speaking to the bartender. Her long, perfect straight dark hair was in a ponytail that brushed against her shoulders.

"But do you think she remembers..." Deb lowered her voice and whispered, "The kiss?"

Alice didn't know how to answer that. On the one hand, she hoped Misty had never forgotten. On the other hand, she...

No, there was no other hand, because there was no erasing the past.

Alice's heart raced as Misty picked up the beer the bartender passed her and turned to the room. Sure enough, she was approaching their table, her bangs falling across her forehead, her hazel eyes meeting Alice's from across the restaurant.

It was hard to tell what Misty was thinking. She'd always kept her thoughts close to the vest, never engaging in debates or arguments. Everyone in the bar could be brawling over politics or religion, and Misty would still sit quietly in the corner, drinking her beer and possibly wondering what all the fuss was about. You never knew what she thought or where you stood with her, which was exactly what drove Alice nuts.

Because, once upon a time, she thought she'd known exactly where she stood with Misty: BFFs, as the kids said these days.

Deb was the first to react, standing up and opening her arms to Misty. "Hey, you, it's about time you came home and saw us." They embraced, but Misty's gaze fell to meet Alice's over Deb's shoulder.

"I know. You're right. It's been way too long. I sure have missed this place." Misty stepped away from Deb and leaned across the table to hug Derek when he rose to his feet. "What's up with you, troublemaker?"

He scoffed and shook his head. "I'm not the one

contracting STDs from groupies, Misty."

"Ew. And that hurts, Derek. Seriously. Plus, it was totally uncalled for. You're still clueless about how to behave in civilized society, I see." She looked at Alice again, wincing a bit before her features smoothed.

Alice realized she had stopped breathing, as if holding perfectly still would somehow keep Misty from noticing her, while she figured out how to react. And what could she do in the middle of this bar, faced with the one woman she had ever really loved, while everyone else watched?

She finally stood and extended her hand, gripping her crumpled napkin in the other. "It's good to see you, Misty." Much to her relief, Misty didn't lean in for more than a firm handshake. Alice knew if Misty tried for a hug, she would step back and that would be the beginning of one heck of a scene. Avoiding unnecessary drama was the first step to making this as painless as possible.

Misty sank into a chair next to Deb and an awkward silence descended until she said, "Where's Nick?"

Glancing around the bar, Alice noticed all eyes on

their table. Even though Misty had strolled into the Whammy Bar as if nothing had changed in the past twenty years – like it was just their group getting together for their usual Thursday night pizza and beer – everything had changed. She was the small-town girl done good, the singer they could hear if they tuned in to the right station on the radio or see in a concert broadcast on TV.

"I was just going to tell them." Deb seemed oblivious to the attention from the patrons around them as she pulled a slice off the pizza tray for Misty and offered her the plate. "All right, so Nick got a job working nights and you're never going to guess where."

"The circus," Derek said.

"Doing kids' birthday parties," Misty suggested before taking a bite of her pizza.

Alice's mind went blank. How the gang carried on a conversation as everyone else gawked in their direction was beyond her. Who did Misty think she was, sitting down as if it was still 1996 and not 2016? And worse, how could she play into the conversation when all she could think about was the one question she'd been asking herself since high school graduation: *Why did you kiss me back and then tell me you were leaving without me?*

"He got a job at a strip club." Deb sat back with her arms crossed over her chest, looking smug.

Derek shook his head. "Now we know you're full of crap. Nick would never do anything like that. I mean, he's a goof and all, but stripping? Is it April Fool's Day? It must be."

"He says the money is incredible." Deb winked at them. "Bartending can be lucrative in the right place, so why not stripping?"

A collective groan rose from everyone seated at the table and Misty shook her head. "So you're totally serious about this?"

"Afraid so." Deb raised her glass of beer and gave everyone a grin.

Rolling his eyes, Derek turned to Misty. "Forget her. She's not funny, never has been. Tell us what it's like being rich and famous, and why you would drag your ass back to this place after all these years."

Alice lifted her gaze to Misty and noticed her cheeks

heat just a bit. If there was one thing Misty had never cared about, it was being rich or famous or getting groupies. At one time, it had seemed like Alice and the music were what she cared about...

"It's a wild ride," Misty said. When she didn't elaborate, Derek sat back and folded his arms. "That's some man pout, Derek."

"Please, you're living the high life, while we never left Calais. We can only live vicariously through you. You can't just walk in here twenty years after leaving and not tell us the whole story."

"That's what E! is for – those true Hollywood stories and stuff."

Before anyone could pry further, two men approached the table. The one at the front said, "Misty Morse, we work with your dad at the rubber factory, and we just want you to know your old man's real proud of you."

"That's right," said the other, "and from what we can tell, he has reason to be. I don't listen to popular music today, but..." The man reached up and scratched at his gray hair. "I mean, I remember you singing the National

Anthem for school games and stuff, and you were really good back then, so you must be good now."

Alice snorted and then tried to cover it by coughing into her napkin. One of the reasons she loved coming to the Whammy Bar every Thursday night was for the local flavor – old-timers who had lived in and around Calais all their lives and had stories to tell. Derek thumped her on the back and she reached for another slice of pizza. She knew Misty would handle the rambling men graciously, because that had always been her way.

"Thanks." Misty rose from her chair and fell into easy small talk with the men. One thing that hadn't changed since high school was Misty's ability to say very little, yet make a huge impact. She always seemed to remember a name, a face, and some kind of personal detail that always made a person feel important.

Sighing, Alice wolfed down her pizza and then shoved her empty plate toward the half-a-pizza that still remained in the center of the table. She remembered that feeling of being the only person in the world who mattered whenever Misty talked to her. That feeling of being special. The kiss that had left her aching with need.

Misty sat after the men went back to the bar and finished her pizza, fending off both Deb and Derek as they teased her about her fame. Alice simply stared at Misty's hands, so lean and graceful from years of playing guitar. She remembered the feeling of those fingers curled through her belt loops on either side of her jeans that night when Misty tugged her close after Alice had brought their lips together… only for Misty to let her go a moment later.

Misty's next comment drew Alice from her thoughts. "I walked here, so I was hoping Alice would hang out with me like she always did after Whammy Bar night, since we're going the same way."

Alice was pretty sure she'd heard wrong, but the flicker of a smile on Misty's face assured her she was serious. Once she had believed they were going the same way, and not just when they walked down the street from the bar to their houses. Now? She'd spent the last twenty years living her own life, moving on because she had learned the only thing she could be sure of was her own decisions.

And she thought she'd let go of everything until Misty came back into her life.

"That's all right. Derek and I need to get home soon anyway. With winter break, we're playing the responsible adults this weekend – dog-sitting for Mom and Dad."

Misty snorted. "You both still live with your parents?"

"Of course not." Derek rose from his chair and stretched. "But it's easier to tag team, considering they've practically got a kennel. They're up to five dogs now. It's ridiculous. But we're both still single, so we've got the time to lend a hand."

"That's pretty cool. It's great that you do that so your parents can take a break. And, hey, I heard you were writing for the local paper. How do you like being a sports journalist?" Misty smiled at him and Derek pointed at her.

"I love it. For so long I dreamed of going to ESPN, but I'm glad I stayed here. Hometown pride, baby! Hey, any chance you'll have time for old friends after the reunion or are you ducking out of town the moment you play the last note next week?"

A slow smile turned up the corners of Misty's mouth as her gaze met Alice's. "I think I'll have plenty of time to hang out and handle unfinished business between the reunion and the concert, and maybe even longer than that."

Oh hell… Alice took a ragged breath. On the one hand, she didn't want to take Misty's remark as a promise of something more than friendship. On the other hand… Well, yes, they did have unfinished business. And Misty was probably right in suggesting that it was best addressed away from the curious eyes and ears of the bar patrons.

Chapter 4

Misty rose from the chair and waited for Alice to do the same. It wasn't that she was eager to get into a confrontation, but she knew she owed Alice one hell of an explanation. Although Alice had always been the logical one of the group, she was also the one with the shortest fuse, probably because she held everything in by deflecting it with humor, until her frustration built up and just had to come out. Like a volcano about to erupt.

The analogy made Misty chuckle. If anyone needed to let go, it was her. Twenty years on the road, countless temptations, and yet she'd never given in to any of them. Because despite all the beautiful, lithe waifs who had thrown themselves at her, no one could compare to Alice, the one person she'd been stupid enough to let slip away. An explanation was long overdue; she knew that. It just wasn't a conversation she wanted to have in public.

She tried not to laugh as Alice took her time rising from the table. "I don't bite," she said in a low voice. Alice tensed and glared at her, but threw on her coat, said goodbye to their friends, and followed her out of the building to the parking lot. The Whammy Bar was roughly a fifteen minute walk to Misty's house just on the outskirts of town. From there, Alice used to keep going another five minutes, just beyond the pond to her parents' place. Misty didn't know what Alice's living situation was now, though – if she was still there in Maple Corner near her parents or not.

Once they were out of the glow cast by the bar's exterior lighting, Misty regarded Alice. As ever, that wavy brown hair gave the illusion of a carefree outdoorsy woman, but she knew Alice was anything but, especially the way she stood with her weight in one hip and arms folded across her chest.

Which was why Misty knew once she opened that can of worms, Alice wouldn't let her off easy.

Still, she also knew they had to hash this out before the reunion tomorrow night or risk a huge scene. Misty already guessed what she could probably expect when she walked into the reunion. Not that she was arrogant or high on herself, but she imagined there would be a whole lot of squealing and excitement when she walked through the door.

"Can we just go over there?" Misty asked, pointing down the street. There was a darkened stretch of road between the Whammy Bar and the woodworks further along County Road.

"You really want to do this outside in the dark, in the cold?"

"Well, the other options involve going back into the bar, going to my dad's house, or going to your house." Misty waved at her to follow.

"Fine. I'll give you two minutes, because I'm not going to freeze my ass off waiting for you to get to the point."

"That's so generous of you."

Alice glared at her and rubbed her hands together. "You want to be sarcastic? Fine. The clock is ticking."

"Then let's go." Misty turned and, as she walked, heard Alice's footfalls trailing a few steps behind her. When Misty turned to face her, she saw that her once-friend had yet to release any tension. Her arms were still wrapped stiffly around her slim body and that's when Alice's words finally had an impact. It was damn cold outside and a shiver rippled through Misty.

"I forgot about winters," she muttered, shoving her hands into the pockets of her leather jacket, an inadequate coat for late December in Vermont. Why hadn't she thought to buy a parka or something heavy?

"Easy to do when you're living it up in L.A., I guess. You didn't think we swapped climates with Florida or something, did you? It's still the same old Vermont, not that you would know that."

Misty rolled her eyes and grinned. "Are you really, really going to be like this with me?"

"How am I supposed to be with you? You act as if I shouldn't be mad about what you did." Alice's eyebrows had drawn together and Misty knew she had better start explaining herself. Fast.

Now or never. Heaving a foggy breath that shook as she exhaled, Misty said, "Alice…"

"Why did you do it?" The whispered accusation was barely loud enough for her to hear, but Misty felt the hairs on her arms stand on end.

"I wanted to see what it would be like before dragging you out into all of that," she answered. "That's all there was to it. And then you were immersed in school and I didn't want to drag you out of college, and then you were pregnant, so I couldn't expect you to drop everything for me once you had a baby."

"Really?" Alice stood with her legs apart, arms still curled protectively around herself. Misty wondered if she was cold out here too, even though she was wearing a jacket over her blazer and blouse with her jeans. "Why is that? Did you want to get out of this town that badly? Did you figure it would be your big opportunity to score with whoever the hell you wanted?"

"You know I never thought like that." Misty glared at her, head tilted to the side and eyes narrowed. "It's a real jungle out there and I didn't want you to get lost in it until I knew I could guide you through it."

"Sure you didn't." Alice maintained her implacable stance and expression. Even when the wind picked up a little, she didn't flinch. "You told me we'd go together – that I'd get a job in a bookstore in Seattle and you'd get gigs. Even if they were in a shithole, you'd sing and play guitar until you were discovered, and I would be there with you every step of the way. It wasn't supposed to be

about getting out of this town and being famous. It was
supposed to be about living our lives together, like we'd
planned since we were fifteen. I was the one who was
supposed to help *you* deal with everything out there. So
what changed between then and graduation?"

Misty went to put her hand on Alice's shoulder, but
Alice jerked away and continued to stare at her. The cold
cut through Misty, but not as harshly as Alice's
rejection.

"I just wanted to know what I was getting you into
first. You were the smartest girl in school – the class
valedictorian. I wasn't about to take away your future
just so you could keep me company while I pursued
mine."

"Well, congratulations. And it took you twenty years
to figure out how to put that into words? Why couldn't
you have told me before you left?"

"I know you, Alice. You would have used every
logical argument possible to keep me from going
without you, and then I would have spent all this time
worrying about you instead of focusing on my end goal."

"And in all those emails there was never an

explanation other than you would know when the time was right. So what's your excuse for the lack of communication?" Alice tossed her hair and said, "Let me see if I can figure it out. You're not actually Misty Morse anymore. Aliens abducted you and replaced your personality. That explains the lack of contact – you lost your ability to interact with humans, even those you've known since your childhood."

Misty's lips quirked, even though she knew Alice's humor was not meant to be funny. "Good one," she answered, "but incorrect."

"Right, so let me try another theory. When I kissed you, I freaked you out."

"Wow. Simplistic and lacking your usual snark."

"Then thrill me with the truth."

Misty glanced up at the darkened sky. She had forgotten how beautiful it was out here, away from city lights and tall buildings. There was a crescent moon and more stars than Misty could have ever crammed on her bedroom ceiling. "The truth," she said, looking down at Alice again, "is that I wanted to protect you."

"I can take care of myself."

Misty heaved a sigh and said, "Of course you can. But it's a real shark tank out there and I didn't want to throw you into the deep end without a life jacket. Living with a struggling musician is not easy and by the time I could legitimately say I was a singer for a living, you had a baby."

"Oh, I see how it is." Alice dropped her arms to her sides. "You didn't think I was capable of doing any of the things we talked about, like taking care of *you* while you tried to achieve your dream."

"You're wicked smart, but you get so emotional…"

"Bullshit!" Alice turned on her heel and strode down the street, back toward the Whammy Bar.

Misty ran to catch up and pointed at her. "See that? Right there. You take everything personally."

"Of course I took it personally. We spent all of high school planning what we would do after. And what happened? I kissed you – just one kiss – and then you told me you were going to leave the next day without me. You left me here to wonder what you were thinking; what you were feeling about me."

"Feelings?" Misty reached out and yanked on Alice's

coat to tug her closer. The sudden stop made Alice stumble against her and they reached out to steady each other. "I still feel the same thing for you as I ever did," Misty said, moving her other hand down to curl her fingers around Alice's belt loops. "I just didn't know if you were ready for more than that too."

"Then apparently I didn't kiss you the way I should have that night," Alice whispered, her words sending a thrill through Misty. They were roughly the same height and their mouths hovered just inches from each other's. Alice's lips parted slightly and she leaned toward Misty. "I've spent the last twenty years driving myself crazy." Alice's voice shook. "Wondering what I did wrong and missing you every day."

"Nothing," Misty whispered, her lips brushing Alice's. "You did nothing wrong. I was just trying to protect you, to keep us from making a mistake. Living out there in some grungy apartment, you working in some minimum wage job while I took gigs in smelly bars. I couldn't let someone like you live like that. I had to keep you safe."

"I thought –" Alice leaned in ever closer "–it was my

job to do that."

Every touch was electric, sparking across Misty's skin. She ached to put her arms around Alice and never let her go. She would stand there all night if it could make up for the crap she'd put Alice through. Alice's lips were soft and giving beneath hers, and Misty groaned against them. Twenty years of sporadic, self-enforced abstinence left her aching. She might not be a woman of many words, but several were running through her head just then. For years she'd told herself once she was back with Alice, she'd not make the same mistake twice. She'd followed that thought all the way from playing in dive bars to headlining big arenas. Now that she was here, getting her second chance, the words that stood out in her mind were, *Don't blow this. Take Alice with you and never let her go.*

Alice's hands slipped around her neck and the kiss changed as she stepped toward Misty, causing her to take several steps backward until her back pressed into the old oak that stood just off the parking lot. When they finally parted, Alice said, "I can handle anything you throw my way."

"I'm sure you can."

"Then are you sure I'm the one who can't handle this or is that just an excuse?" Alice leaned into Misty again, pressing a gentle kiss to her lips. "Tell me the truth."

Misty caught her breath and cast a glance out along the street. The nice thing about her hometown was how quiet it was at night. No screaming fans clamoring for her outside a smoky hotel room, no room service calling her "Ma'am," and no pressure to smile and wave. She could just be Misty Morse, hanging out in small-town New England with her best friend.

"The truth is exactly what I said. Nothing more than that." Misty raised her hand to sweep her bangs off her forehead.

"You need to cut your hair."

"You sound like my manager. He's always telling me how I need to look."

Alice took a step back, her hands falling from Misty's shoulders. "Fine, I'll take what you said at face value if you apologize."

"Apologize? For what? Trying to make sure you didn't screw up your future?"

"Wow. You are unbelievable." Alice's jaw tightened. It was a look Misty had seen on her often when they were kids. "You still did a shitty thing, leaving me here after all the time we spent planning on walking this road together."

"You're right. It was shitty, and you're not the only one who's had to deal with that every day since I left. What do you want from me?"

"Other than the apology? I don't know." Alice averted her gaze. "I guess the first thing is I need to know you're the same girl. Woman. Whatever."

"Of course I am. What did you think I turned into? Standing on a stage in front of thousands of people didn't make me something I'm not." With a shake of her head, Misty said, "I haven't forgotten what it took to pay my dues – the local gigs at the football games and the school dances, then the places I had to play in around Seattle just to get noticed by the right people. Knowing how hard I had to work to get here just makes me appreciate it that much more."

Alice's furrowed brow softened and now she looked miserable. "I could have been there to support you, if you let me," she said so quietly, Misty barely heard her.

"You wouldn't have known what to do with yourself while I was trying to figure it all out," Misty objected. "Trust me, once I met my manager, it was a whirlwind. There was no sitting still."

"The hell I wouldn't." Alice backed away, shaking her head, her face red and her breath coming out in cloudy huffs. "I don't know why you think you need to protect me. Just because I was never the tough girl doesn't mean I can't take care of myself. I guess we'll never know, though. Stay away from me at the reunion, have a great concert, and then get the hell out of my town."

Misty stood there, unable to move as Alice stalked across the parking lot back toward the Whammy Bar. She heard a distant beep and saw Alice open the door of a sleek sedan. The headlights blazed as the car roared to life, and Alice turned out of the parking lot and sped away from the area.

Great going, Misty thought. In the span of less than ten minutes, she'd managed to kiss the woman she'd always wanted, only for her to walk – no, drive – away from her. *It's going to be like that, is it? The reunion is going to be so much fun.*

Dropping her head, Misty looked down at her black boots and said, "Come on, feet, let's go home." After twenty years of working her way into the music industry, she was used to setbacks, both big and small. Alice would come to her just as soon as she calmed down. Misty only hoped it would be before she was supposed to head out of town again.

Chapter 5

"The nerve. The *nerve* of her!" Alice hissed into her cell phone.

"She didn't apologize?" Deb sounded incredulous. "Okay, tell me how it went down."

Turning and propping her elbows on the top of the circulation desk, Alice flapped one hand helplessly in the air before smacking herself in the forehead. "She asked if we could talk, we walked away from the bar, and then she told me the reason she didn't take me with her was because she didn't want me to screw up my future."

"And… that's a reason to still be pissed off at her?" Deb's voice lost its astonishment. "It sounds like she was trying to do the right thing for you."

"I know, but it still wasn't her decision to make. It was my life and my choice. How could she doubt my ability to take care of the both of us? It's not like she's somehow smarter or more capable than me. Tougher, sure, but I can be tough, too." Alice jabbed at the air with her finger. "I used to think it was the kiss that scared her off, but now I'm not so sure."

"Well, I'm not so sure you need to hold this grudge. No offense, but it's been twenty years. You've both grown and changed so much. Don't you think it's time to let it go?"

Alice straightened as a patron walked in and crossed the floor to the stacks. Lowering her voice, Alice answered, "She's going to be here for over a week. It's going to be hard to let it go, knowing she's in town, and especially since I have to see her tonight."

"Well, you're only obligated to attend one function with her, and that's the reunion. After that, you can focus on Christmas Eve and Christmas, and then she'll perform on New Year's, and be gone before you know it. You can pretty much avoid her the entire time if you really can't deal with her being here."

"I… What… Who said I couldn't deal with her?" Alice stammered.

"You sound pretty freaked out, so I'm guessing… We do not shove pencils up our nose. Holy crap, you're sixteen. What makes you think that's a good idea?"

Alice pursed her lips and said, "Uh, Deb? I thought school was out for the year already."

"Sorry. We're doing end-of-year clean-up and extra credit work, which means I get the future 'Animal House' pledges unable to contain their excitement for the break. Their parents must be so proud. See you tonight?"

With a muttered, "Ugh," Alice ended the call and put the phone on the top of the circulation desk. She spun it around a few times as she pondered Deb's suggestion that she simply avoid Misty after the reunion. It was a possibility, sure, but would she have to go out of her way to do it?

"Hey, I'm back."

"Hey, Abby." Alice watched as her co-worker slid behind the desk and offered her a bag. "Thanks for bringing lunch."

"You're welcome. So I was thinking of something for our next episode of *Mom Genes*." Abby perched on the tall stool behind the desk, legs crossed as she patted the long, blonde strands of her windblown hair into place. Abigail Fitch was Deb's first cousin and also a single mom with a teenaged son. She was a few years younger than Alice and had, in some ways, followed in her footsteps from high school to college. The difference was Abby got pregnant in high school and had to work her way through college with a small child.

With children the same age, Alice and Abby had bonded, and Alice helped out with babysitting as Abby got her start with online classes to get her bachelor's degree when her son was still a toddler.

It was their similar life paths and shared love of genealogy that kept them together, now that the diaper days of motherhood were long behind them.

"Tell me," Alice said, opening the bag and peering in at the wrapped sandwich.

"We should interview Misty Morse, of course."

"Misty?" Crumpling the opening of the bag, Alice bowed her head and said, "I don't think that's such a good idea."

"But the director loves the idea and she really wants us to do it."

"Who wants us to do it – Misty or the director?"

"The director. In fact, she was pretty adamant about us getting Misty on the show when I suggested it. It could be good publicity all around, since everyone knows where we work, you know? Think about shows like *Who Do You Think You Are?* that spark an interest in genealogy by featuring stars. Maybe we could do the same thing."

Alice blinked as she tried to tame the thoughts cascading through her mind. "First of all, the people listening to our show already have an interest in genealogy. Second, it's not the director's decision. The podcast is ours. It has nothing to do with the Archives."

"I know, but with a name like Misty Morse in our title and keywords, that will draw her fans to listen, so my point makes sense. The director was also hoping you could get Misty to visit the Archives as well since she's, you know, one of the few famous alumni we have from Calais. Besides, the Morse family was *the* family at Maple Corner. Might be interesting to see if Misty has any memories of some of her ancestors, like if she knew her great-grandparents at all."

Alice turned and walked toward her office. "I'll think about it," she muttered, not caring if Abby heard. When she got into her office, she closed the door behind her and sank into the chair at her desk. Even though the sandwich had seemed appealing when she asked for it, it wasn't so appetizing anymore.

Flicking her hair back over her shoulder, Alice jiggled her mouse to wake up her computer. If one thing could keep her mind off the frustration burning inside of her, it was work.

Except when she opened her email, the source of her frustration was staring her in the face.

She frowned and clicked on the email from her director with the subject line "Misty Morse Interview." The message repeated everything Abby had said, only in more professional terms and with an emphatic closing: "I look forward to hearing your interview with her on your next episode."

Alice closed the message and looked out the window at the parking lot. It wasn't the best view, but at least she wasn't stuck looking at the same four interior walls or the stacks every day. Leaning back in her chair, Alice whirled to face the glass.

The more things changed, the more they stayed the same, as far as she was concerned. The Archives were a place where the methods might have changed over the years – computerized databases and catalogs now, instead of the card catalogs she had pored over as a teenager – but the end desire of patrons was always the same.

Meanwhile, Misty had gone off and become a big star. But the way Alice felt about her hadn't changed one bit.

She closed her eyes and thought about her first reaction when she saw Misty.

Fear.

Fear that things would be too different. Fear that Misty would reject her then and there. Fear that they could never be the kind of friends they once were.

But they couldn't be friends the way they once were, because Alice didn't want that. After seeing Misty again, she knew she wanted something much, much closer than friendship.

That was only a physical reaction, though. What if, as people, we just don't mesh anymore? Alice tapped her fingers against the arms of the office chair.

Misty was, of course, as attractive as ever. More attractive. Sure, she still favored black, which looked fantastic with her dark hair. But gone were the 90s grunge-inspired t-shirts, shredded jeans, and combat boots. Misty still rocked a certain youthful style – the complete antithesis to Alice's body-conscious tops and pants – but it seemed as natural as breathing for her.

Turning back to the computer, Alice skittered her fingers over the keyboard as she pondered her response to the email from her director.

Well, there was no need to respond on a Friday afternoon. Her podcast recorded on Wednesday nights, which meant she had a couple of days to decide how – or even if – she would extend the invitation to Misty. She could think of plenty of excuses to give her boss as to why Misty would decline it. In fact, her boss didn't even need to know whether she asked Misty or not. She could simply tell the director that Misty was too busy for an interview or to stop at the Archives during her visit.

Fingers hovering over the keyboard, Alice considered opening the email again. She certainly wanted to answer it and put the entire matter to rest. Then again, if she answered now, she knew it would be with frustration, and that was rarely a good idea.

She logged out of her computer and rose from the chair, sweeping the bag with the sandwich up off the desk, along with her purse. There was no use having a knee-jerk reaction to the idea. After all, she'd already done that last night. Better to let things take their own course, especially with the reunion tonight.

Alice hesitated at the door as she plucked her coat from the hook. She lingered at the cart of books and manuscripts along the wall just inside her office door, her fingers brushing over the cold metal of one end of the cart. Despite her feelings, she didn't want to have a repeat of last night. Going off on Misty in a semi-private place was one thing. Bitching her out or – worse – snubbing her completely in public was another.

As Liza would say, "That wouldn't be cool."

Tossing her hair, Alice looked up at her closed door. She supposed the only option was to be civil, at the very least. Maybe even friendly. The last thing a celebrity like Misty needed was hometown drama to get back to the paparazzi.

Curling her fingers around the smooth doorknob, Alice turned it and stepped back into the main library area. "Hey Abby," she said, approaching the circulation desk.

"Yeah?" The blonde turned and smiled at her.

"Why don't you bring this home for the kiddo?" Alice handed her the bag. "And I think I'll leave early, since the reunion is tonight."

"Sure. It's a big deal, especially since you need to talk Misty up for the podcast. Oh, and don't forget to see if you can get her to come to the Archives, too."

"Of course." Alice knew she was lying. She wanted to keep her personal feelings from intruding on her professional life, and the only way to do that was by not inviting Misty anywhere, to anything.

"Oh, one more thing. Mr. Stanhope called."

Alice folded her arms and waited. Mr. Stanhope was one of the major donors of books to the Archives. Books, especially those about history and genealogy, were expensive, which mean Mr. Stanhope's steady donations were among the most generous they received.

"Yeah, you know he's distantly related to the Morses, so he…" Abby pitched her voice lower and let out a few gravelly "harrumphs" before continuing in her imitation of the man. "Harrumph, he has a vested interest in hearing that we featured such a prominent family in our work. Harrumph, harrumph."

It was the first time in the past two days Alice had laughed and she took a deep breath as soon as the chuckles subsided. "I get the hint. There's no way out of this."

"Not if you don't want you-know-who up your butt for not doing it and for Mr. Stanhope giving her crap about you not doing it." Abby rolled her eyes and shrugged. "I'm sure it'll be fun."

"Right. Fun." Alice rubbed the back of her neck and looked at the front door. She had once been a person who had fun, especially with Misty. These days, her idea of fun had nothing to do with facing the person who had destroyed their friendship. "I better get going. I don't want to look like I went right from work to the reunion."

"All right. Let me know if you definitely book her for Wednesday night. It's kind of important."

"You'll be the first to know." Alice waved and then shrugged into her coat as she walked to the front door. When she was outside, she let the smile fall from her face. The whole drive home, she distracted herself with NPR. At least listening to other people talk about world issues kept her internal monologue from filling her mind with fears, questions, and more.

As soon as she pulled into the driveway, she called Deb and left her a voicemail. Even though she hadn't eaten lunch, Alice still didn't feel hungry. She hurriedly undressed, chucking her clothes in the hamper, and got in the shower.

Without the radio, she no longer had a distraction. Every thought that went through her mind now was contradictory. *What if she doesn't actually show up? What if she does show up? What if tonight sucks? What if it's better than I expect? What if I really should let go of this grudge? What if we kiss again?*

It was the last thought that was most prevalent in her mind as she toweled off and then stood in front of her closet, trying to choose an outfit for the event.

"Alice?" called Deb's voice from the foyer. "I'm here."

"Oh good. Come into the bedroom."

Deb entered with a chuckle. "Is that an invitation?

Sorry. You're just not my type, being a woman and all."

"Funny and no." Alice gestured toward the closet and pulled the towel tighter around her body. "What should I wear?"

"Good question, considering I came here as soon as I could and haven't even considered what I'm going to wear tonight. My first thought would be clothing." Deb joined Alice in looking at the clothes hanging in the closet.

"So who's running the asylum?"

"My teaching assistant. She's got it handled and the day's almost over, anyway. Hmm…" Deb reached in and took out a sleek black cocktail dress. "What about this?"

Alice shook her head. "Too formal. Besides, it's my go-to outfit for New Year's Eve and fancy dates."

"When was the last time you had a fancy date?"

"Um, never, but it could happen."

"Okay, then." Deb hung it back on the rack. "Why not just go in jeans and a nice sweater? Its casual dress, so how many people are going to bother dressing up more than that?"

"Yeah, but that's boring."

Deb crossed her arms over her chest. "You don't want to go boring tonight? It's just a bunch of people you went to high school with and you've seen most of us since then."

"Well, most of you, yeah." Alice gathered her hair in both hands and tugged it over her shoulder, looking down at the ends. "But, you know, not *all* of you."

"Not all of us meaning Misty. So..." Deb reached into the closet and started going through each hanger, one by one. "Tell me more about what happened outside the Whammy Bar last night."

Eyes focused on her hair, Alice muttered, "Stuff and things."

"Stuff and things sounds to me like something you don't want to talk about."

"Well, if you must know, I got down on one knee, professed my love for Misty, and then we made out until the cows came home."

"Are you sure that wasn't a dream you had? Most of the cows are indoors these days, since it snowed."

"Shut up." Alice tossed her hair back over her

shoulder. "Just help me find something that looks…"

"Sexy as hell?"

Alice ground her teeth. "Non-matronly."

After digging through the closet, Deb tossed Alice a dress and said, "That. I've never seen you wear it in public."

The slightly shimmery dark red fabric was crisp in Alice's hands and she gave it a gentle squeeze just to hear it crinkle. "I wore this to my dad's retirement party, before he and my mom moved to Arizona."

"So it should still fit."

"I don't know. That was about six years ago and I just never got rid of it. It might be too…" Alice held the dress up against her body and narrowed her eyes at her reflection in the full length mirror. "Too quirky for a reunion."

"Are you kidding? It's adorable." Deb got on her hands and knees on the floor of the closet before slinging one shoe and then another across the room. They landed in the opposite corner. "Wear it with those."

"Mary Janes? Don't you think I'm a little old for those?"

"If you're too old for the quirky dress and the Mary Janes, why did you hold onto them?" Deb shook her head. "I remember a time when you were one of the cutest, quirkiest girls in school. Not like Misty – she rocked. She was like our very own Joan Jett. But you weren't stuck in your turtlenecks and jeans all the time, the way you are now. You wore adorable dresses and shoes, and never cared what anyone else thought. So why don't you think back to a time when you weren't all about being Ms. Responsibility?"

Alice sat on the bed, the mattress bouncing with her as she dropped against it. "I don't know if I can. It's not something I wanted to become, even after I had Elizabeth, but it feels like it was pushed on me. Other people decided they knew what was best for me and I just kind of let it happen."

"Other people meaning Misty?"

Alice nodded. She couldn't stop the sniffle or the blinking as tears burned at her eyes. "She fucking rejected me and her whole excuse was because she couldn't let someone as smart as me go ruin my life, living with the uncertainty we would have faced every day by moving cross-country. It's such bullshit. I can take care of myself. I think I've proven that over the past twenty years, raising a kid on my own for sixteen of them."

"Of course you have." Deb sat next to her and draped her arm over Alice's shoulders. "I don't know any woman stronger or more self-sufficient than you. You kick ass and that's why you need to go to this reunion."

"To kick Misty's ass? I think we're a little old for using violence to solve our problems." Alice dabbed at her eyes with the heels of her hands.

"No, although that would be entertaining. Throw in some mud for the benefit of the guys."

Alice finally let out a laugh.

"But what I mean," Deb continued, "is show her how strong you are by forgiving her and letting go of the past."

"I don't know if I can do that."

"Why not?"

Letting out an uneven breath, Alice looked up at the ceiling for a moment. Then she lowered her head and plucked at the edges of the towel.

"Because when I saw Misty the other night, I
realized I'm still in love with her."

Chapter 6

Misty hung back outside of the restaurant where the
reunion-goers were already celebrating. Looking through
the windows she saw conservatively-dressed women
leaning in for "Oh my gosh, it's been forever!" hugs and
kisses, and men in sports jackets high-fiving each other
as if they were still teenagers, instead of adults with jobs,
kids, and the usual day to day responsibilities.

Her breath crystallized on the cold air, brief particles
of condensation that vanished just as she exhaled again.
It had been her brilliant idea to dress as if she were going
to perform at one of her concerts – a red sleeveless,
asymmetrical lacy top that contrasted with her favorite
black leather jacket. She'd drawn the line at the leather
pants, though, and chosen a pair of slim-fitting black
slacks with a nice crease.

A glance at her watch told her she was fashionably
late – the reunion had begun thirty minutes ago – but
even though she arrived ten minutes ago, she hadn't seen

any sign of Alice.

Resigned, Misty flipped open her compact mirror to check her reflection one last time. There was no use in waiting to make her entrance. It would, she knew, cause a stir. While having international fame and people treating her with deference made her queasy, being among old friends should not cause the same discomfort. She pushed away from her father's car, and stuffed the keys and compact in her zippered jacket pocket. Unlike most women, she wasn't much for carrying a whole bunch of stuff on her. One pocket usually held her cell phone and keys. The other held the compact and a lip balm. Misty liked to think of herself as "low maintenance" and let stylists handle the looks she was expected to sport on stage.

Each step of her chunky-heeled black boots brought her closer to the double doors of what she figured was the nicest restaurant in Montpelier – the perfect place for an upscale high school reunion. So much for the casual dress aspect of it. She shoved both doors open and grinned. It was something she loved doing – passing through double doors as if entering an old-time saloon.

Sure enough, heads turned her way. Misty paused for effect, a tactic drilled into her through years of high school drama camps and by PR people. It gave onlookers a chance to realize who she was before she continued, whether she was crossing a room or a stage. The two women at the table covered with nametags smiled up at her. Misty tried not to judge people, but she knew her perceptions were usually spot-on. These were Pinterest moms – concerned about looking perfect from their whitened teeth to their Coach bags. She imagined they each had a copy of the latest Oprah's Book Club selection on their bedside tables and fancied themselves deep thinkers for reading it.

She didn't begrudge them that, of course. She just knew the type. They were usually the moms accompanying their teenaged daughters to a concert and Facebooking selfies from it, and Misty knew she owed moms like them a huge debt of gratitude for everything she had achieved.

"Misty Morse, what an honor to have you here," the bubbly blonde with the *Jersey Shore*-style poof in her hair said, pressing her hand to her chest as if she couldn't control the flutters of her heart. "You must be the most successful person in our entire class. It's so cool that you could make time for us!"

Misty swept her gaze over the woman's nametag and smiled. "Dana Manning, you haven't changed at all," she said sincerely. It was true. She remembered Dana from their high school days – head cheerleader, the quarterback's girlfriend, and smarter than most people gave her credit for. "Thank you for all the work you did putting this together. It's great to come back and see everyone."

"Of course, of course! It's not like it's a long drive from Boston. That's where I live now. I'm a meteorologist there and a mommy, of course. Did you know my daughter is on the national cheerleading team?"

"Wow, that's impressive," Misty said, hoping she sounded more enthusiastic than she felt. Sports remained beyond her scope of interest, but she knew being on any national team was a big deal.

"Well, you know – like mother, like daughter. Ah, here you are." Dana twittered like an excited bird as she ran her fingers along the rows of nametags on the table and plucked one from the middle. "April, check Misty Morse off the list."

The other woman at the table gave Misty a similar megawatt smile and said, "Check!" in a much-too-loud voice. "My daughter is so excited about the concert next week. How fabulous that you're going to stick around to do that for our little town."

Misty accepted the nametag and affixed it to the lacy top, just beneath her leather jacket. Her stylist would have a fit if she put a hole in one of her costumes, but she figured lace was already full of holes and there was no one here to tell her what to do – for once – so it hardly mattered.

"I'm looking forward to it, April. After all, it's my little town, too." It had been the right thing to say, because both women managed to smile even wider. Before Misty could think of something else to add, a fresh breeze blew through the room and she looked up to see the person standing at the door.

Alice Cavanaugh, as beautiful as ever and, Misty thought, looking quite pleased with herself.

And why shouldn't she, when she looked absolutely smoking hot in the red iridescent taffeta dress with the black Peter Pan collar and black Mary Janes. Misty bit back a "Holy shit" as Alice removed her coat, revealing the sleeveless, fitted bodice and letting the full skirt swing as she walked.

"Happy twentieth reunion, ladies," Alice said, approaching the table with a catlike smile.

Misty lifted her gaze to Alice's hair. Instead of loose waves, it was gathered at the back of her head in a relaxed ponytail that allowed it to tumble along the slim length of her neck. A laugh bubbled to her lips. She had decided to avoid her own usual ponytail and let her long, straight hair fall loose.

"Well, Alice Cavanaugh, you certainly don't look twenty years older." Dana handed her a nametag while April inked another checkmark on her list.

"Thanks. It's the Botox. I made sure to get it done all over my face." Alice turned to Misty, her green eyes alight with a twinkle that reminded her of their high school years. The early and mid-90s, when all they cared about was making mischief, music, and big plans.

Misty vaguely heard Dana whisper to April, "Botox all over the face. Don't forget that."

"You look like you need a drink." Alice twined her arm around Misty's and led her past the check-in table, then turned her down a short hall just beyond it. "Coat room first, but don't get all frisky with me just yet. The lipstick is still fresh."

She spoke so fast, Misty had to do a double take.

This was the Alice she remembered. Not embittered or angry, but perky as heck and throwing people for a loop with her blithe, hard-to-read remarks.

"Did you really get Botox?" Misty asked as she waved away the hanger Alice offered her.

"Please, do you think I would do that? No thanks. I don't want frozen face syndrome. Hang up the damn coat." Alice waved the hanger at her again.

"Um, keys, phone, all that is in my coat."

"Oh, right. I forgot we live in the coat theft capital of the world." Alice reached out and drew the coat off Misty, draped it over the hanger, and placed the hanger back on the rack. Misty suddenly felt very exposed with her bare arms. Even though the restaurant was warm, a brief shiver claimed her. What was with Alice just stripping her like that? "There we go. You drinking or not tonight?"

The music in the restaurant cranked up, drowning out Misty's throat-clearing. Drinking was the last thing on her mind as Alice stood here in front of her, looking so damn perfect. "We need to figure things out," she finally said.

"No, we need to get through this reunion without causing a scene, so come with me." Alice yanked on her arm, but her hold gentled as they moved from the coatroom to the restaurant. "For now, let's pretend June of 1996 didn't end the way it did. Can you do that?"

Misty nodded. Her heartbeat was still elevated, though, as she and Alice walked with their bare arms tangled together. In a way, it was like old times, but there was something heavier in the air between them. Resentment bubbled just beneath the surface of Alice's perky good nature, flavored by something else Misty couldn't quite pinpoint.

"Good, because I came here to enjoy a night with old friends. We're going to catch up on shit with everyone and like it, damn it. And you'll let me protect you by making this as non-eventful as possible." Alice dragged her to the bar and rattled off an order. "I hope you do shots," she told Misty.

"I don't drink much of anything."

"That's good, but sometimes a girl has to treat herself. It's like swearing. Do it less often, so when you actually do it, it'll have more of an impact." Alice slid her money across the bar when the bartender brought the glasses and a bottle of whiskey. "Thanks, Mateo." She poured the drinks without spilling a drop, even though the liquid flowed nonstop from one glass to the other.

"How did you learn to do that?" Misty asked, taking the shot glass Alice handed her. It was ice cold in her hands and she realized then her skin felt blazing hot, like it was radiating fire. She wondered if her skin looked as hot and flushed as she thought it must, but kept her focus on the glass in her hand. The whiskey would just burn its way down her throat, adding fuel to the fire.

"We only watched *Cocktail* five hundred times when we were kids. It's not that hard. Here's to broken dreams," Alice said, raising her glass.

Misty lifted her eyebrows. "Chasing dreams."

"Achieving dreams."

"Sweet dreams."

They both drank and set their glasses back on the wooden bar top with a clatter. "Again?" Alice asked, picking up the bottle.

Misty looked at the empty glasses. It might be nice to have a little bit of a buzz after all. "Just one more."

The whiskey flowed again and this time, Alice seemed to have softened a touch. "Here's to opportunity."

"To taking chances."

"To second chances." Alice looked at her and Misty could have sworn she saw tears swim in her eyes, before she blinked them away and smiled again.

"To second chances," Misty whispered and they both tossed back the shots.

"Oh yes, yes, yes." With short little pushes, Alice inched her empty glass toward the opposite side of the bar. "That takes the edge off. So, who do you want to see first? Everyone is going to want a piece of the great and powerful Misty."

Misty shrugged, leaned back against the bar, and surveyed the room. Most of the people there were casting her glances and whispering to their friends. She could guess what they were thinking and saying. "That depends on who's here."

"Everybody, for the most part. I think the only ones who couldn't make it tonight were, um, Mick and Nora Davies. He's assigned overseas right now and she just had a baby, so they weren't up for the travel."

"Wow, they're still together?"

"Check your Facebook, prodigal daughter." Alice turned and her dress swooshed with the movement. It caught Misty's eye and she lowered her gaze.

Alice had always had the best legs in school – slender thighs that tapered down to her knees, and then gently curved calves that again narrowed into fine ankles and delicate feet. There were times all Alice had to do was walk by, leaving Misty unable to think straight as her gaze fastened on those perfect legs.

"Fine," Alice said decisively. "We'll work our way around the room clockwise. That's probably the easiest way to make sure you see everyone and do the catching-up thing. Otherwise, you're going to have the entire class of '96 clamoring for your attention."

"And then what do we do after this?" Misty asked, letting Alice take her arm once more. She was accustomed to letting others take the lead – the PR people, the execs, her manager – something she'd always hated about stardom. This was different. She felt relaxed in Alice's capable, familiar hands.

Alice's eyes focused on her face without blinking. "That is going to depend on a number of factors, but I'd like to think we'll peacefully go our separate ways after tonight."

"Is that really how you still feel?"

"Why shouldn't it be how I still feel? You're the one who left after that kiss, not me." A hint of the bitterness crept into Alice's voice as she spoke.

"But I made the decision before it happened, not because of anything you did. If I had known we both felt the same…"

"You did know after I kissed you, though, didn't you? Why didn't that change your mind?"

Misty dropped her gaze and looked at the subtle

patterns in the plush beige carpet beneath her feet.

"What a stupid question. You could have, but you chose not to change your mind."

"Non-refundable ticket," Misty muttered.

"Some things are worth more than money. Hey, it's Emily Woodsmall. Em!" It seemed the subject was dropped as Alice led Misty around the room, reintroducing her to high school acquaintances. The entire time, the music was a bit too loud for meaningful conversation, but everyone got their opportunity to gush over Misty's appearance. It wasn't long before every woman had expressed her admiration and every man had made some sort of ridiculously flirtatious remark to her. Soon, groups of party-goers migrated from the main restaurant to other, smaller rooms just off of it.

Whoever was controlling the music finally turned it down enough for people to talk without yelling and Misty breathed a sigh of relief. She had enough loud music in her work. She didn't need it when she was supposed to be relaxing.

The restaurant finally opened the buffet to them and Misty piled a spoonful from every chafing dish onto her plate. She noticed Alice did the same as they walked to the table they had chosen. "You still eat enough," Misty pointed out.

"So do you."

"Being on the road makes me hungry."

"Being me makes me hungry." Alice waved and Misty turned to see Deb and Derek approaching, with another man just behind them. She leaned toward Misty and whispered, "Now we can get the full scoop on Nick."

"The stripping thing?" Misty let out a snort of laughter and looked at the food piled high on her plate. "He was always such a clown, I can't imagine any woman wanting to shove dollar bills down his underwear."

Alice's faced scrunched in disgust. "Ew, I don't want to think about him in his underwear, period. But you're right. What about the class clown could possibly appeal to the ladies?"

"Maybe he strips at a gay club," Misty suggested.

"No way. Nick would not go for that. He's way too hetero."

"Too bad. He's probably missing out on a good time."

This time it was Alice who snorted before pressing her hand over her nose to stifle it. Misty's heart melted. She missed this – her best friend happy, joking, and laughing with her. It was a magic she could never recapture by email, especially after ditching Alice the way she had. And, yes, she had to admit to herself that she had ditched her. How was she going to say those words out loud to Alice, though? How could she bring herself to acknowledge it and give Alice the apology she had demanded, not to mention deserved?

"Guys, you remember Misty," Alice said as their friends approached the table with their food.

"Considering it's been only about twenty-four hours since we last saw her, I think that's a safe assumption. I'm glad you're here, Misty. It's just like old times." Deb settled in the chair on the opposite side of Alice.

"Me too," Misty said, perhaps too emphatically. This was so much better than striding through a hot nightclub, nodding to fellow celebrities, and getting the best table in the house. It might have been the whiskey that helped relax her, but she realized it was more than that. It was the comfort of being among old friends who liked her for her.

Deb removed her utensils from her cloth napkin, laid it over her lap, and nodded at Nick. "So why don't you tell them what's going on, since we missed you at the Whammy Bar last night."

Nick was just as Misty remembered him from high school – a too-skinny, too-tall guy with almost gaunt features and a shock of brown hair that flopped over his forehead. He rolled his eyes and said, "In front of her? No way."

"Deb already outed you at the Whammy Bar last night, so you might as well come clean," Alice said, scooping mashed potatoes onto her fork.

When Nick bowed his head, Misty reached out to pat his arm. "Man, you don't have to say a word, if you don't want to. Look, no one is going to judge you."

"Are you kidding? I'm going to," Deb said, chortling.

"No," Misty said firmly. She glared across the table. "I like you guys, but no one is going to judge him. Let him live his life. He's doing whatever he wants or needs to do. Don't give him shit for it."

Alice and Deb exchanged glances.

"People do things – sometimes things other people don't understand or think are stupid or malicious," Misty continued. The room suddenly felt much too warm and her words tumbled out in a rush. "Sometimes those things come from a place of fear or pain or need, so we should let it go and move on. If the other person wants to talk about it, they'll talk about it. And they may never be ready to talk about it, but until they are, just let them be. Are we clear?"

"Crystal," Deb drawled. She looked down and cut into her chicken without another word.

Alice held Misty's gaze for a moment before she looked at Nick and then Derek. "I feel like there should be pitchers of beer on these tables, instead of water and iced tea. Who decided on this kindergarten set-up?"

"Right?" Derek's nod was emphatic. "I'm going to hit the bar and get us a pitcher. Does anyone want anything in particular?"

Everyone shook their heads and he left the table. An

uncomfortable silence settled until Alice said, "So Misty, what's next after your visit?"

Misty was grateful to her for redirecting the conversation, but it was a question she couldn't answer just yet. Should she be honest or give a noncommittal answer? "I'm… not sure," she finally hedged. "My manager and the label take care of those things." There. At least it was partly true.

Except, this time after being home and away from the pressures of her work, she wasn't sure she wanted to let anyone else take care of anything. How could she explain to everyone that she wasn't just there for the reunion, but there to see if there was a reason for her to stay?

"Oh, that makes sense. Do you ever know your tour schedule ahead of time?" Alice asked.

"Sure, but I'm enjoying this little hiatus for now. And winter isn't really the best time to tour anyway. I mean, plenty of bands do it, but I try to get the label to avoid sending me on tour when people might have to deal with snow to get to a concert or have more important things to spend their money on, like Christmas presents. It just doesn't seem fair to the fans."

"That's awful nice of you," Nick said. He looked a little more at ease now that the conversation had shifted away from him and he smiled at Misty. "So I guess you're living the dream."

"Not really, but there's a lot more to this life than just being able to travel and make music." Misty looked across the table at Alice, who tilted her head inquiringly. Good. She was interested. That meant Misty could finally talk to her, finally get everything out in the open between them.

Derek returned and set a pitcher of beer in the middle of the table with a flourish, then flopped back down in his chair and shook his head. "That Dana Manning still looks like she could bust my balls. They should make a horror movie about women like her – 'Night of the Middle-Aged Cheerleaders' or something like that."

"They do get scarier with age, don't they?" Deb agreed.

"And some get better with age."

Misty realized belatedly that she had spoken aloud, her gaze fastened on Alice as she had. Fortunately, Dana had a mic in her hand and she wasn't afraid to use it.

"Hi everyone!" she called. "Welcome to the twentieth reunion of the Union 32 Class of 1996! Our small town hasn't seen much by way of change, but our graduates sure have."

As Dana rattled off the list of alumni names and accomplishments, everyone applauded. Misty knew Dana would mention her last in the roster of classmates and, sure enough, a burst of applause followed her name. Misty rose and smiled at the people gathered in the room, acknowledging everyone before she sat back down to her dinner.

Misty cast another glance at Alice. The more the reunion went on – the music, the reminiscences, the people – drawing them back to 1996, the more she remembered her own pain one May night, only a few days after their prom. The pain she had kept inside all these years.

"I don't like it." *Alice had folded her arms, looking defensive.*

"What do you mean you don't like it?" *Misty felt like she couldn't breathe.*

"I don't like it," her friend repeated. "It's not quite… you. It sounds like a sold-out version of you."

Closing her eyes for a moment, Misty tried to shove the memory back to the recesses of her mind, but it refused to leave her alone. Last night, Alice seemed determined to hold on to her anger, and Misty had thought her completely unreasonable for it.

Now, though, recalling her own pain from twenty years ago, she knew they were both dealing with only half the story. She rose from the table with a muttered, "Excuse me," and strode to the coat room, leaving her half-eaten meal behind. She couldn't afford to let her feelings show in there – not when she was going to be in town another week and might run into anyone. Making a scene at the reunion was the last thing she wanted to do.

Instead, she tugged her coat off its hanger and thrust her arms into the sleeves, then barged through the doors. The fresh air whipped against her face and she took a moment to breathe it in, to stabilize her emotions.

"Hey," came a voice behind her. "Hey!" She turned to see Alice jogging toward her. No coat, though. She was just in that terribly gorgeous dress that made her look like something out of her wildest dreams. "What was that about?"

"I screwed up."

"What?" Alice folded her arms and stared at her.

"Look, I screwed up – I admit it. You hurt my feelings and I took it to heart, then I turned around and hurt you."

"I... I hurt your feelings?" Alice sounded stunned, her voice catching in her throat. "What the hell are you talking about?"

Misty squeezed her eyes shut and clenched her fists at her sides. This was not supposed to be how she behaved. She had avoided the temptations of stardom over the years, relying on her cool head to keep her from getting in too deep with drugs, gambling, groupies – any number of things she could have lost herself in and chose not to.

"It hurt when I wrote the song that you didn't like and I realized I could handle critics, but I couldn't handle you not liking my music. Your opinion... mattered too much."

Alice remained silent and tense, her arms wrapped

around herself as she stared at Misty.

"What if I wrote something that I loved, that I knew my fans would love, but you didn't like it? I cared way too much about what you thought and I was afraid of letting it get in the way of the music."

"So your music had to come first." Alice's head bobbled as if she wasn't sure whether to nod or shake her head.

"Yeah, it had to, and I didn't want your feelings to get in the way. You know I pour my heart into what I do."

"I know, yeah. I guess…" Alice shifted her stance and rubbed her hands up and down her bare arms. "I guess I just thought maybe you could pour your heart into me, too. But the music meant more to you than our friendship did."

Misty's mouth hung open. What could she say to that, when she knew she had already confirmed the truth of the accusation?

"I see." Alice's voice was bitter.

"I didn't mean it like that."

"You know what? Maybe it's better everything came

out the way it did." Alice shrugged as she backed toward the restaurant. "At least now I know where I stand – in your shadow, like always."

Misty watched her retreat, and then turned back to the parking lot with a hissed curse. The fear and pain she had carried with her had been justified, but she finally knew that her betrayal wasn't.

Chapter 7

"Mom. Your phone won't stop buzzing."

"Then kill it with fire," Alice muttered, bowing her head. Even though no one at the reunion seemed aware of the scene that had played out between her and Misty in the parking lot, she was acutely aware of it. People spent the night asking where she'd gone and Alice would simply shrug and say something sarcastic, brushing them off. Misty hadn't returned and Alice had pretended not to care until she got home and cried into her pillow.

After all this time, she was supposed to be numb to any mention of Misty. But so far both times they met up ended in a fight with no resolution. She wished everything would just go back to the way it was – that she could just carry on as if Misty had never come back into her life.

"Holy shit, Mom. Answer it."

"Watch your mouth."

Liza thrust the phone under Alice's face and waved it in front of her. "I will if you stop ignoring Misty's calls."

Yanking the phone out of her daughter's hand, Alice grimaced at the number. "How do you know it's Misty?"

"It's an L.A. area code. Plus, she sent a zillion text messages."

"You read my messages?"

Liza's mouth twisted in a guilty grimace. "Just one."

"Well, crap. How did she even get my cell number anyway?"

"I don't know, but I'm sure she has her sources, like mutual friends or something. What happened last night?" Liza sank into the chair opposite her mother's.

Alice propped her elbows up on the kitchen table on either side of her cup of tea, so she could look at how many calls and texts had come in between last night and now. Six calls. Thirteen text messages. Misty certainly was persistent. Alice thumbed through the first few texts and then deleted all of them. She wouldn't even bother to listen to the voicemails.

The problem was Alice finally realized the mistake had been made on both sides of their friendship. But Misty's reaction by choosing to leave for Seattle without her was still uncalled for. They should have talked about it the way they had talked out so many other things in their lives back then.

"Hindsight," Alice muttered, laying the phone face down on the table.

"That's helpful. Could you be anymore vague?"

"Sure. Obtuse, even."

"Mom," Liza whined. "I'm so lost. I wish you would just tell me what's going on here. You usually tell me everything."

Alice rested her head against her hand. "You're too young to understand. We certainly were, which is what got us into this mess."

"I'm still not following."

"Good. Go do your homework."

"Um, I'm on winter break."

Lifting her head, Alice stared at her daughter. "Right. So... do winter break things. It's Christmas Eve and all that."

Liza regarded her for a moment longer and Alice got the uncomfortable feeling that her daughter could see everything that had happened the previous evening – that she wore it like a neon sign. "Okay," Liza finally said. "I do have some new tracks I want to play with. I guess I can wait until tonight for the explanation you owe me."

"What explanation?"

"The one you promised me a few days ago. You said you'd tell me all about you and Misty when we did our annual Christmas Eve movie marathon. A few hours shouldn't make a difference, but if you're going to be stubborn, I can wait."

Alice bit back a groan. She remembered now and she wondered which boots she should wear to kick herself for making such a promise. "That reminds me – we need goodies for tonight."

As she pushed the chair back from the kitchen table, Liza wagged a finger at her. "Way to change the subject, mom, but you're not getting off that easy."

"Not changing the subject. Just realized we need to get the junk food. Play with those tracks. Make music. I'll go buy the fun stuff."

"Please remember the Sno-Caps. You always forget them."

"Yuck." Alice glared at her. "That's because they're like weird bumpy chocolate nipples."

"Mom, ew!"

"Just saying." Spinning on her heel, Alice plucked

her purse off the peg where it hung on the coat rack. "Any special requests besides bumpy chocolate nipples?"

"At this point, my only request is that you stop saying 'bumpy chocolate nipples'," Liza retorted.

"Well, you know I can't promise anything." Alice opened the front door and slid through the opening before whatever her daughter chucked across the room hit it. She was halfway to Montpelier when she realized she had left her cell phone on the kitchen table. Still, considering the only person intent on calling her was Misty, it was no loss.

She started her errands by purchasing some last minute gifts for Liza and then visited Delish Monteplier's Sweet Shop for as much candy as she could get to the front counter. As she walked out of the store, two bags heavy with treats draped over her arm, she saw a tall, slender figure approaching from the other end of the street.

No one looked quite like Misty with her long, straight hair flowing beneath a wide, round hat, her lean body clad in black jeans, a t-shirt, and the black leather jacket that was, as usual, open despite the chill in the winter air.

"Have you considered dressing appropriately for winter in Vermont?" Alice asked when she was close enough to read Misty's t-shirt. It was white with black grunge-style screen print letters that simply said "PUNK."

"I have, but I like to live dangerously." Misty tilted her head almost coquettishly and Alice took a step back.

"Are you... flirting with me?" she asked.

"Maaaybe. What's in the... Oh, the candy store." Misty lifted up on her toes and craned her neck as she peered into the bags.

Alice yanked them behind her back. "Sorry. These are only for the initiated."

"And what does it take to be initiated?"

"Other than passing through my vagina, you must be part of a long-standing Christmas Eve tradition."

"We had traditions once. We could always work your vagina into them."

Heat radiated through Alice's body at Misty's words. They certainly did have their own traditions, yes.

Whether it was Alice being at every single rehearsal for an event or being the first person to hear Misty's songs, it had once been a prominent part of her life. As they stood on the sidewalk, regarding one another, Alice wondered if there was any way to bring it back.

Instead, though, she pushed the thought aside and asked, "So what are you doing out here?" The heat seemed to have settled in her cheeks, but she could blame the chill in the air for that if Misty had anything to say about it.

"I needed to get Christmas presents for Dad and I'm also avoiding calls from my manager. He's kind of a pain my in butt these days. I know, you probably think I'm crazy for wandering around downtown without a cell phone on me, but I can't take it anymore."

"You too? Sounds like karma to me, considering all the calls I've been getting from you since last night."

Misty chuckled and bowed her head. "Yeah, I guess so. Sorry about that."

"Also, your shirt really isn't… right."

"Hm?" Misty looked at her again.

Alice gestured with her free arm. "The 'PUNK'

shirt? Really not you. You're more… I don't know. Folksy sort of indie rock."

"You've listened to my albums?"

"Your songs, at least, and it's kind of hard not to when they're on the radio. Not that I wanted to, but my daughter is a fan, so I've caught snippets here and there."

"Ah. Right. Well…" Misty stared at her shirt so long, Alice wondered if maybe she had upset her by critiquing it.

Should she make a joke about it or would that just be rubbing in everything from last night's argument?

"I should remember my roots," Misty said. "I mean, I started off with grunge and punk, but my sound has definitely matured since then. It's still very much about standing against the norm, though, and going your own way."

When Misty looked at her, Alice warmed all over again. "Really?" she asked. "I haven't listened that closely. Um, my daughter has, of course, but she wants to get into the music industry."

"Interesting." Misty's body was so tense, Alice

wondered if she was feeling awkward or just cold. She had her answer when Misty said, "Look, its freezing out here. I have to admit I'm stupid for not preparing better to spend a week where winter actually exists. Can we go somewhere warm and talk? I feel like we should discuss what happened last night and the night before that."

"And twenty years before that?"

"Please?" Misty asked.

Alice let her eyes fall closed as she considered Misty's request. If they didn't get this out of the way and they ended up bumping into each other constantly, the next week had the potential to be beyond awkward. Plus, there was the question of whether or not she really wanted to hold on to a twenty-year grudge. It seemed ridiculous and juvenile when faced with the person she had once stuck with through *everything*. Even if Misty hadn't stayed with her, Alice supposed that was no reason to go on being angry.

"Come on," she said. "Capitol Grounds has incredible coffee and breakfast sandwiches." Alice motioned for Misty to follow her along the State Street storefronts and led her into one only a few doors down from the sweet shop.

When they were seated with cups of hot coffee and their orders placed, Alice waited for an opening. She had to bite her tongue as the urge to dominate the conversation filled her, but she knew she had to let Misty take the reins. Otherwise, all she would do is blurt out her issues and she had already done that. Twice.

Alice never had a problem leading a discussion, but she knew Misty's reticence all too well. As kids, Misty was the least likely to initiate a confrontation, even if she had a bone to pick with someone. And as a woman, she apparently still needed to learn to speak up for herself. Alice supposed it didn't help that their generation received conflicting messages that told them they could be anything they wanted to be, but for a woman to speak up for herself equated to being aggressive, bossy, and bitchy. So Alice waited, giving Misty a chance to get the ball rolling.

Misty lowered her coffee cup and said, "This is good. Thank you for letting me talk to you."

"You're welcome. You're not going to get hounded by groupies or anything?" Even though the restaurant was fairly quiet, Alice wouldn't be surprised if a gaggle of besotted teenaged girls somehow managed to suss out Misty's location and bombard her with requests for autographs.

"No, I'm not *that* big of a deal."

"Sure you are. You saw how everyone at the reunion reacted when we did our circuit. They love you."

"No, Alice, I promise you I'm not." Misty put her hand up and said, "Don't argue with me. I just want to talk about us right now. What you said last night about always being in my shadow surprised me. I didn't know you felt that way."

Alice felt her heart flutter with anxiety. So they were finally getting to the crux of the matter. She supposed they would have to, if they were going to work their way beyond it. "You were…" She drew a long breath. "You *are* so creative, so talented, so amazing, and when you decided to leave without me, I looked back and wondered if maybe I was just like some loyal puppy dog following you around. Maybe we weren't ever really friends. I was just your first groupie."

"Don't ever think like that." Misty reached across the

table and curled her fingers around Alice's wrist. Her touch was still a bit cool, but it sparked something in Alice. "I never thought of you like that. Alice, you were always my better half. You're the one who's smart and driven. I wanted things for myself, but I could never match your level of intensity."

"I could never match your talent."

When Alice met Misty's gaze, they were both smiling.

Alice's next words came out in a rush. "I just wanted to be with you."

"And I just wanted to be with you."

"I mean forever and as more than a friend."

"I got that from the kiss." Misty's fingers moved from Alice's wrist to her hand. "Do you still feel that way?"

They parted as their server brought their food, Misty's hand lingering over Alice's before she drew it back across the table. When they were alone again, Alice said, "So much has changed over the years, but I don't know if that's one of the things that has. I mean…"

Alice hesitated, fumbling with her words. "I know I've

been in love with you for a long time and it hurt to take a chance and get rejected. Did you really think I would get in the way of your music?"

"I thought it was a possibility. Maybe you felt like all you did was sit in the corner and nod along while I played guitar and sang, but I took your opinions to heart."

"Shit." Alice looked down at her sandwich, still not quite sure if she was ready to eat it. The conversation had helped them get so much out in the open, but it still felt unfinished, as if they were only scratching the surface. "I didn't want to hold you back in any way. You know that, right?"

"I know you didn't and that's part of why I made the decision I did. I didn't want you to come with me and for us to lose what we had. What if you decided you hated living with me or we butted heads on things that mattered to us? I felt like we were still too immature to make that kind of decision – to live together. Besides, like I said, you have this incredible mind and I didn't want to rob you of what you could have by staying here."

"Like an education my parents were willing to pay for?"

"Precisely."

"And an unexpected pregnancy?"

Misty pointed across the table. "As far as I know, I had nothing to do with that."

A laugh finally escaped Alice and she shook her head. "Not unless you grew some new body parts and changed your name to Bill."

"You had a one-night stand with someone named 'Bill'? Oh, Alice. I am disappointed in you."

"Well, I had spent pretty much my entire college career focusing on academics and pining for you, so it seemed like the best way to break my rut." Alice picked up her sandwich and finally took a bite out of it. It was the first time in days she had felt truly hungry and she wondered if her stomach thought it had some catching up to do.

"But you never dated guys in high school," Misty pointed out, before picking up her own sandwich. "I think most everyone accepted that they didn't have a chance with you, even if you didn't tell anyone outright about your sexual preference."

Alice swallowed and shrugged. "Sexuality wasn't exactly a big thing when we were growing up, remember? I mean, very few people came out as gay, even if it was obvious they were. I'm sure you remember Tim Moore."

"Of course I do. I sat behind him in home room and I saw him last night at the reunion."

"Right. With his husband."

"Hm." Misty nodded. "I guess we always knew, but we never really did discuss stuff like that in the 90s. You're right. Especially being a small town and all."

Alice set her sandwich on the plate and lifted her coffee cup to her lips. She realized it did feel good to finally get everything out in the open with Misty, to discuss their past and, perhaps, move on with their futures. "So, yeah, I didn't exactly run around telling everyone I was a lesbian."

"Neither did I." Misty stared at Alice. "How come we never told each other, though?"

"That's a good question." Alice threaded her fingers together around the cup, cradling it as if for comfort.

This was one of those moments she couldn't count on her intense, talkative nature. Because her damn heart was complicating her ability to think. "I kind of thought you already figured it out back then. I think I was pretty much in love with you from the moment we met, but by the time I realized it in high school, I was afraid of scaring you off by telling you that. What about you?"

"Same thing. There were days…" Misty's pale cheeks blossomed a lovely pink and Alice grinned.

"You're blushing. What are you thinking?"

"Nothing." Misty brushed her aside, but Alice's own heart was racing.

"I have to know," she insisted. "Please."

Misty pushed her sandwich around on the plate. "There were days I wanted to ask you to marry me."

"Before it was legal?"

"Even if we had to find a local Wiccan to perform our wedding, yes."

With a smirk, Alice said, "Handfasting, you mean?"

"Mmhmm."

"Why didn't you ask?"

"And mess up our friendship? No thanks. I thought

maybe it would be enough to just be together, but I also knew if we left together – if we lived together – things would get a heck of a lot more complicated." Misty leaned back in her chair, finally looking her in the eye once more. "I blew it by not thinking we could handle a life together. I left and you felt betrayed. My fear was all I could hold onto at the time. My fear of what being together would do to us and the futures we both wanted for ourselves."

Alice felt her lips quirk into a half-smile. "And I'm the intense, smart one? It sounds to me like you were doing some serious overthinking back then."

"I was, but that was then. This is now." Misty licked her lips and Alice realized she was seeing a side of Misty she had never seen.

The singer was nervous. She of the calm, cool, and collected was actually uneasy. It made Alice glad she had assented to her request for a talk. Maybe they were making progress.

"I'm sorry for doing that to you." Misty's voice was low, but firm. "It was the shittiest thing I could do to you. Probably the shittiest thing I've ever done in my life, dumping you as a friend just because I was scared to lose you. I've regretted it every day from the moment I left Calais without you."

Alice mirrored Misty's previous gesture, reaching across the table and taking her hand. "Thank you for your apology. I forgive you and I'm sorry if I gave you any reason to doubt the strength of our friendship or my belief in you and your music."

"Thanks." Their eyes met and Alice felt her shoulders finally relax, the tension draining out of her body. The grumbling of her stomach broke the silence, killing the moment. Misty chuckled and pushed at Alice's hand. "I think we better eat."

"Yeah, we better." Alice withdrew her hand and picked up her sandwich. They ate in silence, only this time it was a comfortable one. Alice finally felt something she hadn't felt in twenty years. Peace. Not only that, but there was something else there, too. It was a nostalgic sensation – the two of them, together, oblivious to everything around them. The world was just Alice and Misty again, inseparable friends. They belonged together, like pieces of a puzzle. Alice's heart swelled with happiness.

Misty was back and they could start over again.

"Okay, so I get that you did the sex thing with the Bill person out of boredom or maybe it was a wild party thing–"

"Wild party thing," Alice confirmed. "Decompressing from finals and all that jazz."

"–so is that why you weren't safe about it? Were you of the 'My uterus is invincible' mentality? You were always so much smarter than that."

"I guess I went through my stupid stage, like any twenty-something. I mean, I'm a smart person, just like you said. I know basic biology, so what came over me that I just ignored the possibility?" Alice shrugged and waved at the server. "I think I just wanted to not think too hard about something for once. The sex wasn't great, but I can't deny it was worth the end result."

They ordered fresh drinks from the server and Misty leaned back in her chair. "So you sound happy about motherhood. It must be a real trip. Tell me about the kid."

"Elizabeth – well, everyone calls her Liza – is

sixteen and she wants to produce music. She must get it from her father, because she certainly doesn't get any musical or creative talent whatsoever from me."

"Does she know her dad?"

"Oh, yeah. I mean, I didn't want a relationship with Bill or anything, but I also didn't want to deny Liza a father and Bill a daughter, so I stayed in contact with him until Liza was old enough to do it herself. They're really good about writing and calling each other. They visit each other occasionally, too. He and I aren't buddies or anything, but we're on good terms. I never ask him for anything, but he's maintained a college savings for Liza and contributes to things like household expenses or special things she wants to do, like extracurricular activities."

"That's really cool of him," Misty said.

Alice nodded in agreement as the server brought another round of frothy coffee drinks. "He insisted. I think that's the way it should be, if possible. Anyway, with a kid there wasn't time for me to have a love life, so I just spent those first several years working and raising her. Mom and Dad helped out with babysitting until she hit ten, and that's when they retired to Arizona."

"Nice. I remember they always talked about living somewhere warmer."

"Yup, they're New Englanders, but they were ready for the year-round warmth. I'd follow them if I didn't love this little town so much." Alice glanced around Capitol Grounds and a shiver raced through her. "I honestly don't know how anyone can leave here. I mean, look at this place. So much history and all that New England beauty. And you really can't beat living in a small town near a big city."

"Yeah. I've… missed it…" There was a wistful note in Misty's voice and Alice watched her circle a finger around the rim of her coffee cup, before raising it to her lips.

It was hard to believe anyone could trade a small town life for one of glamor and stardom, and want the former back. When Misty didn't elaborate, Alice decided not to press her. Yet. Instead, she said, "Tonight's mine and Liza's annual Christmas Eve movie night. Do you want to come over and watch with us? I've got enough candy and junk food to make us sorry for a week." As soon as the words left her mouth, she wasn't sure why she'd said them, but it felt right.

"That sounds really bad for a number of reasons."

"I know. We might have to have our stomachs pumped because of all the sugar. Wild times in small town Vermont, you know. It's your chance to become a part of our tradition."

Misty spread her arms and said, "If the vagina is included, I'm in."

Chapter 8

Misty followed Alice to her house and looked up as they pulled into the driveway. It looked like a newer home than most of the ones in Calais, with its pristine white siding and dark blue accents. She stepped out of the car, a sedan borrowed from her father, and stood in the driveway for long moments, before she said, "When did you buy this place?"

"When Liza was little. I lived with my parents for a while and they helped out a lot, but that got crowded by the time Liza was in kindergarten." Alice rummaged through the backseat of her car for her shopping bags. "Things got even more crowded when Liza became a teenager, but at least here we can put space between us."

"I'm sure she's a great kid." Misty had never met Liza, let alone seen her or heard much of anything about her.

Alice gave her a significant look. "I'm sure we were great kids too, but we had our moments and so does she. Look, if she gets all giddy and doesn't leave you alone, don't be afraid to tell her off. She wants to be a music producer, so she'll probably hassle you with questions. I can tell her to back off from the get-go, if you want."

"No, no." Misty put her hands up and shook her head. "I'd love to answer any questions she has. I'm not sure how helpful I can be, since I'm on the other side of the actual production process, but I like helping kids with musical dreams. It's the one thing I can say I'm super proud of in my work."

They walked through the door and Alice set her bags on the island that separated the living room from the kitchen. Misty loved how open the house looked, while still feeling welcoming and relaxed. There was a large screen TV in one corner, a gas fireplace surrounded by a stone façade, and a Christmas tree set up in front of a large bay window.

"This place is gorgeous." The only place Misty had called home for the past twenty years was a variety of hotel rooms and a very exclusive condo that she liked well enough… But it wasn't the same as coming home to her father or a place like this.

She leaned on the island and watched Alice put the food away, and then tuck the gifts at the bottom of the pantry closet. What would it be like to live here, to come home to this place every night, knowing it was permanent and someone would be waiting for her?

An idea that had teased at the edges of her mind ever since she started planning the trip reappeared and she wondered if it was feasible. It was contingent on so many things, though – Alice's friendship being the main one.

"Okay, the only thing left is to make the dinner." Alice set various ingredients on the counter next to the stove. "Every year, I make Pad Thai for Christmas Eve. It's our favorite dish. Do you like Pad Thai?"

"I don't know."

Alice hesitated and turned to her, hands clasped around two bottles in an overhead cabinet. "You don't know? They don't feed you on the road?"

"Of course I eat," Misty said, rounding the island and pulling out a chair at the kitchen table. "Not the way you do, though. I lack the iron stomach. It's just that I've never tried Thai food."

"Never tried Thai food? Have you been living in a bubble? Are you the amazing bubble singer?"

Misty snorted. Alice could almost always find a way

to poke fun at everything. None of the people who surrounded her – her manager and the label executives – did that. They were all about money and hype. There was no time to kick back and relax when you were managing a superstar.

Right now, she knew they were still freaking out that her contract with the label was up at the end of the year and Misty still hadn't signed the new one. It was one of the reasons Misty had to get out of her dad's house, away from both her cell phone and her dad's home phone. Both seemed to ring nonstop, her cell phone blowing up with texts and emails reminding her that the clock was ticking. All she wanted to do was shove the new contract up her manager's butt.

The more time she had away from all of it, the more she realized it wasn't just nostalgia, or love for her family and friends that brought her home. She was tired of feeling enslaved to the label and to her manager's expectations of her.

She traced the patterns in the table's wood surface. It was another piece that fit so well into this cozy New England home – a thick oak tabletop and white legs with matching chairs. Alice moved comfortably throughout the kitchen, keeping up a steady chatter about old classmates, both those who had come to the reunion and those who had missed it. She finally turned to Misty and leaned back against the counters.

"Your life must be so different than everyone else's." Her voice was low, quiet, and Misty wasn't sure what Alice felt as she spoke. "Do you ever regret the decisions you've made?"

Ah. So that was it – a question that got to the heart of the matter.

Misty cleared her throat and said, "Besides the regrets I've already admitted to? Sometimes. But it's not regrets so much as realizations now."

The silence stretched between them as Misty waited for Alice to take the opening she had given her. Before Alice could speak, a girl entered the kitchen and trilled, "Oh my gosh, it's Misty Morse!"

Another girl followed and stood right behind her. This second one was, Misty realized, had to be Alice's daughter. There was no mistaking the long, wavy chestnut hair or green eyes. "Yeah, she's a close personal friend of my mom's."

"Misty, I have all your records!" the first girl gushed. "Can I get your autograph?"

"Doofus. What's she going to sign for you?" Liza nudged her friend. "Just bring a CD to the concert, so you have something for posterity."

"Are you doing signings after the concert?" the girl asked.

Misty smiled. "That's the plan," she said. "Why don't you tell me your name and I'll make sure I have something special waiting for you."

"Oh my gosh, oh my gosh, oh my gosh!" The teenager jumped up and down and squealed, then turned and clasped Liza's hands in hers. "Did you hear that?"

"Yeah, I haven't gone deaf yet, but keep screaming and I'll get there."

Misty bit back a laugh. Clearly, Liza had her mother's sense of humor, as well as her good looks.

"Wow!" The girl twirled back to face Misty. "I'm Tori Cavanaugh. I'm Liza's second cousin."

"Tori, I'll remember you."

Liza shoved at her cousin's shoulders and said, "And

134

on that note, it's time to go."

"But…" Tori protested as Liza pushed her toward the door.

"You've got to go home because your parents are expecting you, and Mom and I have our Christmas Eve movie marathon after dinner. Sorry."

"That's mean. You're hogging Misty all to yourself!"

"Please. Would I do that? You know Mom and I have our traditions and they are not for the uninitiated."

"Yeah, I know, but…"

Misty heard more adolescent arguing and then the sound of the front door closing. When Liza returned to the kitchen, she looked sheepish. "Sorry about that," she said, extending her hand. "It's nice to meet an old friend of mom's. I'm Liza – Elizabeth – her daughter."

"It's nice to meet you too." Misty shook her hand. An aroma filled her senses and she inhaled. "Wow, that smells so good."

"Mom's Pad Thai is the best you'll ever have, other than Pad Thai made by people who actually know what they're doing. Are you staying for dinner?" Liza's eyes were soft with hope.

"I did invite her," Alice said, stirring the food in the wok. "She's never had Thai food, so we really can't let her go on without trying something. I thought we could let her peek in on the Cavanaugh Christmas Eve tradition, since we know she'll never tell another living soul."

"Awesome, and then you'll be one of the initiated." Liza sat in the chair next to Misty's. "I hope you like Christmas movies."

"I do. Do you watch the classics, like *White Christmas* and *It's a Wonderful Life*?" Misty asked.

"Ha, are you kidding? That's amateur stuff." Liza shook her head and gestured toward her mother. "She picks the cheesiest movies possible, the Hallmark crap. They're cringe-worthy and hilarious and sweet, all at the same time."

Misty compressed her lips into a thin line and then said, "You still watch that stuff?"

"Hey, it's funny." Alice's defense was half-hearted. "Every circumstance is implausible, yet somehow ends perfectly. It makes for great made-for-TV mockery.

Christmas Eve should be filled with laughter and food."

"I guess that makes sense." Misty exchanged glances with Liza, who grinned. "And you share this enthusiasm."

"Mom has taught me well," Liza intoned, winking.

"Oh dear..."

With a dismissive wave, Liza shrugged and said, "I love it. Just us girls. It's great. Nothing against guys, but I can't imagine my father or boyfriend enjoying this sort of thing."

"What boyfriend?" Alice asked. She removed three plates from a cabinet next to the stove.

"The one I plan to get when I get out of this town and meet someone worth getting. So, Misty, you need to tell me what it's like."

Misty darted her gaze to Alice and then back to Liza. "Well, I can't tell you what it's like to have a boyfriend..."

"Oh, I know that. I mean getting out of this town and making music."

"Well..." Misty tried to think of the best way to answer Liza. Kids weren't idiots, she knew that, so gentle honesty seemed like the best policy. "The getting out of this town part isn't all it's cracked up to be, but making music is wonderful."

Alice caught her glance and quickly dipped her head, thrusting her spoon into the pile of noodles in the wok.

"I know mom told you I want to be a music producer," Liza said. "I want to make music and hear it on the radio."

"Why not sing or play in a band?"

"Please." Liza scoffed as Alice set plates of steaming food on the table. "I'm not talented like that, but I have an ear for mixing harmonies and melodies. I've made loads of samples and actually DJed some of the dances at school."

Forks clattered against the table as Alice dropped a handful of flatware and then set cans of soda in front of their plates. "So any advice you have on Liza's career path would be appreciated," she said, sliding into a chair.

Misty looked up at her and took a moment to just appreciate where she was. Considering Alice's anger toward her, she didn't expect them to be able to move forward as friends without some bumps in the road. But she was glad they were on that road. Her heart swelled with those old feelings of love for Alice – her loyalty, her honesty, her warm presence. As a teenager, Alice had been all angles and hard edges. As a woman, there was something softer about her. Misty wanted to curl up with her and get to know the new Alice.

"I don't necessarily want to go to either L.A. or New York," Liza said, drawing Misty from her reminiscences and thoughts. "But I know I've got to get started as soon as I finish high school, pay my dues and all that. Mom and I already discussed skipping college entirely and getting straight into the industry."

"You know it's a very from-the-bottom-up career field, right?" Misty asked. "Also, college could benefit you. It's important to understand music theory, for example." She popped open her soda and watched as Alice did the same. Except Alice put her lips to the rim of the can and gently sucked away the droplets that had flown out of it. Misty wondered how those lips might feel on hers again. Kisses certainly seemed to soften Alice even more…

"Yeah, I know and I'm okay with that. What I'm

trying to figure out is the best place to start – which coast."

As she twirled her fork in the noodles, Misty tried to formulate a response. Of course, the major cities were the places to be, but she wondered just how good Liza was, how much potential she had. She also didn't want Liza passing college by just because she thought she didn't have anything to learn.

"Um, that's not spaghetti," Alice pointed out.

"What?"

"You don't need to twirl it and gather it like pasta. Just shovel it in your mouth." To demonstrate, Alice stuffed a forkful of the Pad Thai in her mouth and mumbled, "See?" around the food.

"That is so gross," Misty said.

"That's Mom." With a shrug, Liza did the same, filling her mouth with the noodles. "You should try it."

Rather than cram the noodles into her mouth, Misty took a delicate bite of the food. It was better than anything she had tasted in a long time. Then again, it was homemade, and no one had made her a homemade meal since… Whenever she came home, she took her father out to eat or brought take-out. He didn't cook too much and he kept it pretty simple when he did.

"This is amazing," she told Alice. "I've never had anything like it."

"Good. Maybe you'll come back more often if I make your mouth happy."

Dryness claimed her throat and Misty let out a choking cough.

"Nice going, Mom." Liza thumped Misty on the back. "If she dies, it's on your conscience."

"Like so many things in this world." Alice's wry response only made Misty cough harder, unable to laugh properly.

When she finally recovered, thanks to a few sips of soda, Misty wiped tears from her eyes. This hearty laughter would be the death of her, Liza was right, but what a wonderful death it would be. "Seriously, thank you. This is great. I wish you could cook for me all the time."

"You're welcome." Alice looked at her, green eyes softer than usual and that was when Misty once again saw the girl she remembered. The girl she always dreamed of kissing, but never had the courage to, until graduation night when Alice leaned in and started it. She had never forgotten those lips against hers – sudden, velvety, and searching.

She lowered her gaze to the food. It really was better than anything she'd had, even at the fanciest restaurants in L.A. or while visiting other major tour venues. It wasn't long before the three of them had scraped their plates clean and gone for seconds, which finished off the entire batch of Pad Thai.

"Okay, are you ready for the snackening?" Alice asked. She gathered the plates and flatware before Misty could even offer to help with the dishes.

"As long as you got my Sno-Caps," Liza said.

"You mean your bumpy chocolate nipples? I got them."

Misty sputtered and clapped her hand over her mouth.

"See what you've done again, Mom? Jeez, she laughs like it's new to her."

"Well, she wasn't a big laugher when we were kids. Were you, Misty?" Alice was rinsing the dishes, but she turned to look at her friend.

"No, I suppose you're right. You could always make me laugh, though." It was true. Even the goofiest class clown's shenanigans hadn't fractured Misty's calm, cool exterior. But Alice's fast-talking wit and way of turning statements around on people elicited snorts of laughter from Misty more often than not.

This time when their eyes met, Misty wanted to find a way to turn the tables – to make Alice let out a laugh, a joyous peal that let her know everything was right between them.

Instead, though, she stood and stretched. "Dare I ask what's up first?"

"Bathroom break while we get the junk food together," Liza said. "And if you don't have a strong stomach, I suggest taking a few of the antacids you'll find in the medicine cabinet. That will help you get through the night."

"Do you even have room to eat anything else?"

"Of course I do. Mom's been training me for this since I was young. Eating is our Olympic sport."

Misty refrained from pointing out that Liza was still

young and eating was the antithesis of sports. Instead, she craned her neck and peered at what she figured was the hall. "Bathroom's that way, I guess?"

"Yeah. Go for it."

By the time Misty emerged from the bathroom, Liza had laid out popcorn, chips, wasabi peas, and candy. Misty popped a wasabi pea in her mouth. "You have a thing for Asian foods," she remarked.

"Yup, and cheesy movies and eating way too much." Liza fell onto the couch gracelessly before kicking her feet up on to the one edge of the coffee table that was free of snack food. "What do you do when you're not on tour or cutting an album?"

Misty sank down on the cushions and furrowed her brow. What *did* she do between commitments while she was all alone in her pristine, silent condo? "I just write more songs." Not that she'd been inspired to write much of anything lately…

"Really?" Liza wrinkled her nose. "That sounds kind of miserable. I mean, no offense, but don't you have any friends?"

Misty shook her head. "No time for them, really, and

it's kind of hard to know who to trust when you're a celebrity. It feels like people who say they want to be my friend are usually in it for something."

"I can see that. What about outside interests or connections back here?"

The sigh that escaped her was heavy with twenty years of regret. "I used to have the best friend in the world," she finally said. "Someone who kept me grounded and kept me from getting lost in my music by reminding me to look outside of it. I still need someone to do that for me, now more than ever."

When she looked up, she saw Alice standing by the sofa, the remote clutched in her hand. Misty could guess her thoughts. *You made your decision.*

"I guess…" Liza looked up at her mother and then back at Misty. "Things just change, sometimes."

"They do, yeah, even if you wish they hadn't."

Chapter 9

Try as she might, Alice couldn't ignore Misty's words. How could Misty wish things hadn't changed? She had fame, fortune, and a life that revolved around music – everything she had wanted when they were teenagers.

But maybe it wasn't all it was cracked up to be.

Or maybe, just maybe, she really did miss Alice.

Alice had to admit she still wasn't quite sure of Misty's sincerity. After all, didn't fame change a person? Didn't it cause them to turn their backs on everyone they cared about? As much as superstars talked about "staying grounded" in those stupid interviews or never forgetting where they came from, she wondered how much of that was true and how much was just lip service, in order to appear approachable to their fans.

"So the first movie is something about some big city woman getting trapped in a small town over the holidays and falling in love," Alice said, trying to ignore the way her heart warred with her mind. Without any more explanation, she turned on the movie and sat on the couch on the other side of Liza. She didn't know if having her daughter as a buffer was necessarily fair, but for now it gave her some space.

As the movie went on, Alice felt her heart and breathing settle back down into a normal pace. Misty and Liza both seemed oblivious to her tension, and she was grateful they had struck up an easy chatter, passing the candy and snacks to each other, and laughing at inappropriate times at the movie.

The next movie started ninety minutes later with only a brief interruption and Alice finally reached for food now that her stomach had stopped turning somersaults. Clearly, she and Misty still needed to talk about their past and, if Misty's hints were any indication, their future.

No, not their future. Just *the* future.

Right?

She finally worked up the courage to look at Misty. To her surprise, Misty was already looking at her over Liza's head, and the expression on her face brought Alice back to 1996.

That kiss. The look on Misty's face when they first

parted.

She felt it too.

Then why had she left? And why wasn't her answer good enough for Alice?

Because I was in love with her and she broke my heart.

"Earth to Mom." Liza's hand waved in front of her face within inches of Alice's nose.

Alice blinked and realized she had been pouting, her lips pursed with frustration, as if she was reliving her reaction to Misty's news after the kiss.

"You haven't touched any of the snacks."

"I just ate popcorn."

"Yeah, like one piece. You usually scarf the popcorn like there's no tomorrow and leave none for me."

"But there is a tomorrow and Santa needs her rest."

Liza's brow furrowed. "Santa? Mom, really? I'm sixteen, not six."

"Actually," Misty interjected, "your mom did get some last-minute gifts she probably needs to wrap."

Liza looked even more perplexed. "What is this? Two movies, you don't eat, and then we're done?"

"It's not that, honey," Alice said. "It's just that I have things to finish and there's still so much catching up I would like to do with Misty. Like, twenty years' worth."

"Yeah, I suppose I can dig that…"

"So when this movie is over –"

"Say no more." Liza rose from the sofa. "I'll be in my room, watching something else. You two catch up and maybe work out whatever happened back then, because I may not know the story, but I'm not a dumb kid. Something went wrong and I hope you two can fix it, because it would rock to tell everyone my mother's best friend is the one and only Misty Morse."

After Liza left, Alice rose and gathered bowls. When Misty followed suit, picking up the empty candy boxes and turning off the TV, Alice said, "You don't have to do that."

"Don't I?" Misty blocked her way to the kitchen. "I have to do so much more to make up for being such a shitty friend."

"Fine." Alice capitulated. They had to dig deep and hash it all out sooner or later. "Let's do this." She followed Misty into the kitchen and as soon as everything was either tossed in the trash or recycling, or settled into the dishwasher, she leaned back against the counter.

"Liza's a good kid," Misty stated.

"Yeah, tell me something I don't know."

"And pretty perceptive from the sounds of it."

Alice tried not to smile at the compliment. "You don't know the half of it."

"Does she know you're...?"

"Yeah. I mean, she never asked or anything, but I just told her straight up."

Misty pointed at her and winked. "Cute. Nice pun."

"Well, I wanted her to understand why her dad was a one-time thing and why I wouldn't be searching for a daddy for her. Kids get to an age where they realize the standard family unit consists of a mother and father, so I decided to just tell her the truth – that families are diverse and don't have to adhere to that standard." Alice gave a one-shouldered shrug. "She's fine with me being gay, if that's what you're wondering."

"That's great."

"Yeah. But I know you didn't come in here to talk

about my kid, so where should we start?"

Misty scuffed the sole of her shoe along the tile.

"Well, I'm sure you haven't gotten out all of your feelings about things between us, so where do you want to start?"

Alice swallowed. It was now or never. She could carry twenty years of resentment beyond this night or get to the crux of the matter.

"I loved you – was in love with you – and when I tried to let you know my feelings, you…" Alice paused, her voice catching in her throat. "You broke my heart and I don't think I can ever get over it."

There it was – the unvarnished truth. The thing she should have told Misty in the few emails they had traded before the lines of communication were severed by time and bitterness.

"I loved you too. I still love you." Misty maintained her distance, but Alice saw her body tense.

"I feel the same way, but we've both changed." Alice lifted her shoulders and shook her head. "Where would we even start?"

"Well, I know I need to start with an apology," Misty

said. "The one I gave you earlier was inadequate. So I'm sorry for all the pain and hurt I caused you. What I did as the worst thing possible. I blindsided you and went back on my promises. I behaved like an asshole, just because of stupid insecurities, and I've spent all these years regretting it. I can't take back the pain I caused you and the pain I suffered doesn't make up for it either, but I'm sorry."

"Why didn't you explain any of this in an email or something back then?" Alice asked.

"Well, I didn't feel like I could. You know me, and by the time I was ready, I was on the fame train and you were pregnant." Misty lowered her gaze to her shoes. "Our lives moved in totally different directions and dragged us even farther apart. That's no excuse, though, because I started it. I accept the blame entirely." She pressed her hands to her chest and her eyes misted with tears when she looked at Alice. "I have no excuse but fear – fear that the music would come between us and then we would end up hating each other."

Alice curled her fingers under the edge of the counter. She wanted to accept the apology, but she knew she had her own apology to offer first. "Fear held me back, too, you know. It kept me from asking why you left. I thought I could pretend I wasn't hurt and just move on. But I was hurt, and…" Her voice thickened and she sniffled in an attempt to hold back her own tears.

But it was too late and the tears flowed, tracking hot, wet streaks down her cheeks.

"I'm so sorry." Misty took a step forward and, in an instant, Alice was in her arms, crying against her shoulder.

Alice nodded, her head rubbing along Misty's neck as she did. It felt good to cry it out – the anger, loss, resentment, and regret of twenty years. There was no getting it back, no reclaiming the past, and Alice accepted that.

"I hated you," she mumbled into the fabric of Misty's shirt, "and now I forgive you. I really do."

"Good." Misty stroked her hair, still holding her close. "Maybe we can start fresh with each other."

"I'd like that." Alice knew she should pull back, but here in Misty's embrace she felt like she was home.

"Alice." Misty shoved at her a bit. "Alice."

"Mmm?" She didn't want to leave the warmth of Misty's presence. Not just yet.

"You got my sweater all wet."

Even though she didn't want to, Alice broke the embrace and grinned. "You deserve it. I hope you smell like a herd of wet sheep for the rest of your life."

"Because that's attractive to the groupies."

"Very. I'm turned on already."

"Shut up." Misty gave her another little shove and Alice chuckled. Everything felt right again – the weight of the world lifted from her shoulders now that her best friend was back in her...

Wait.

Rather than let her fears build up again, Alice folded her arms and asked, "Sooo... Where does that bring us now?"

"Well, I've got another week here, so why don't we hang out together and see. But not 'just like old times.' I mean, let's focus on getting to know each other. Let's catch up on everything about us."

"That's a pretty tall order. How do I even explain the last twenty years? Motherhood has been a major part of it."

"I know, so we better get started."

As they sat in the living room in front of the fireplace, in the glow of the hearth and the lights of the Christmas tree, Alice told Misty everything she could think of from graduation until the present. Misty helped her wrap the gifts and fill Liza's stocking with goodies.

"It feels like there wasn't much to tell after all," Alice admitted as they placed the presents under the tree and hung the stocking from the mantle.

"Maybe not to your way of thinking, but having a kid is a big deal. And if you're happy with your work and your life, then it sounds like you're living the dream."

Alice stepped back to look at their handiwork. It was the first time another person besides her parents had helped her prepare for her daughter's Christmas and it felt wonderful. "I suppose so. Really, the only thing that's been missing in my life is someone to share it with." She held up her hand. "Please don't take that as something against you – I just mean in general."

"No, I understand what you mean."

"Good. Hey, would you like to see where I work?

The director mentioned she would love to have you visit the Archives and it might be fun for you."

The smile that tugged at Misty's lips let Alice know she was glad to be asked. "Fun in what way?"

"Well, I could dig up some family history for you to look at, if you'd like. The Morse family is pretty well documented and I bet we could find some interesting stories."

"I'd like that."

Good. One request down, one to go. "Great, and can I ask a favor of you that's kind of relevant?"

"A favor? What is it?"

"Well…" Alice glanced up at the ceiling as she tried to figure out how to explain herself. "Don't laugh at me, please, but I have a podcast with a co-worker. A genealogy podcast, actually, called *Mom Genes*, and we were wondering if you would like to be a guest."

"Why me?"

Indeed, why her? Alice knew her director's reasoning for making the request was purely selfish. She wanted publicity for the Archives and Montpelier in general. "Because," Alice said, "we both know the

Morse family was one of the first to settle the Maple Corner village in Calais, and it's that long history that people might be interested in."

"Oh, jeez." Misty ruffled her bangs with her fingers. "I don't know anything about my family history, you know that. Whatever you find will be news to me. Genealogy and research and all that stuff has always been your thing."

"I know, so maybe that's why a visit to the Archives would be a good idea. We could spend Monday or Tuesday seeing what we find and then record the show on Wednesday, like we always do."

Misty continued to fidget with her hair, smoothing it and then inspecting the ends. "Who's this 'we' – you and me?"

"Yes, as well as my co-host, Abby."

"Oh. Is she…"

"She's a single mom, like me," Alice explained, "and straight, so don't get any ideas. She's just a co-worker and a friend. So what do you think?"

"It sounds like fun, as long as we don't spend the entire time talking about how famous I am." Now Misty was wrapping her hair around her hand, unwinding it, and wrapping it again. Alice realized there was definitely something up with the reigning Queen of Cool, so she pulled out a chair from the kitchen table and sank down into it.

"Why don't you tell me why you feel that way?"

"Are you a shrink, now?"

Alice laughed and used her foot to pull out another chair. "More like a very concerned friend. Do you ever talk to anyone about this stuff, like the pressures of being famous?"

Misty moved around to sit in the chair Alice offered her and shook her head. "No. Not even my manager, Rick. He thinks I should be on cloud nine, but…" She heaved a sigh, her shoulders rising and falling with the breath. "But I don't even like what I have – the fame. It's terrible. I can't really confess that to anyone, because I'm supposed to be happy, right? But I'm not happy. I'm not even content."

That was unexpected. Alice knew all Misty ever wanted to do was make music and get paid for it, but surely being at the top of her industry was also what she aspired to.

"Really, I can't keep going like this." Misty finally took her hands away from her hair and leaned forward, resting her elbows on her knees. "It's too much. I'm tired of it. I've been tired of it almost from the start."

Alice tilted her head and watched her. "Then why did you stick with it for so long, if you don't mind me asking?"

"I don't know. I guess because I felt like I had no other choice, but to go along with the momentum of it – like it was all I knew and all I had."

"That's not true."

"It's not?" Misty looked at her, eyes full of hope.

"Of course not," Alice whispered, closing the distance between them. "You always had me. Even after you left, no matter how angry I was, I hoped you would come back someday."

She leaned forward until her lips pressed against Misty's. The scent of Misty's shampoo, the curtain of hair falling around them, the nearness of her best friend – it was like nothing had ever changed.

Except where that first kiss twenty years ago had

been a hasty, passionate one, this one was slower. Alice took her time moving her lips over Misty's and thinking about how it felt. Misty's lips were fuller than hers and parted slightly under the gentle pressure. And then she kissed back, her hands curling over Alice's shoulders to hold her in place.

There wasn't anywhere else Alice would ever want to be in this moment. Twenty years of their relationship was long gone and she had to accept it. Misty was here now and they could just move forward together. How Alice hadn't fallen in love with anyone else over the time that passed, she didn't know. Maybe it was because she knew deep in her heart that Misty was the most exceptional person she would ever have in her life.

"Wow." Misty breathed out the word as they parted, Alice giving her enough space to catch her breath, but not pulling away from her warmth just yet. Not that she could anyway, with Misty's hands still draped over her shoulders. They felt heavy there and Misty didn't seem inclined to remove them. "Wow," she said again.

"I waited a really long time to…" Alice shook her head. "Actually, I'm not sure if I ever wanted to try that again, but I'm glad I did. You're not going to run off on me again, are you?" She hated putting herself out there, exposing her vulnerability, but it was a question she had to ask.

"That's something I'm still figuring out."

"What do you mean by that?"

Misty dipped her head so their foreheads touched. "It means everything I said about my regrets isn't just me complaining. I've been seriously considering making a major change in my life and career, but I had to know if it would work – if I would be welcome back home before I took it a step further."

The hour chime of the grandfather clock in the front hall dinged and Alice felt Misty's hands tighten over her shoulders. It wasn't late just yet, but it was getting there.

"I need to wrap presents too," Misty said. "It's the first time I've been home for Christmas in a few years and I know Dad is happy to have me home."

"How come you never reached out to me when you came back here the other times?" Even though she tried not to show it, Alice couldn't suppress her disappointment. Her brow furrowed and she pulled back to face Misty.

"Well, first of all, my time was limited. There was no way I could do the visit justice. Second, I really didn't know what to do or say. When I was in my twenties, I was an idiot. I don't think I started to figure out what I needed to do until I was at least thirty-five. That's when it hit me hard that I was totally unhappy."

"Right." Alice shook her head and then nodded. "I mean, of course not. That makes sense. But I still wish you'd come and seen me. You could have talked to me sooner. Why didn't you at least try?"

Misty straightened in her chair and cast her eyes downward. "For a number of reasons, but mostly because I was being an idiot. I was scared of you rejecting me after it looked like I rejected you. Which, please understand, I didn't. But our lives went in completely different directions – what would a new mom with a baby want with a rock star ex-best friend? Or a mom with a kid in elementary school want with someone who travelled around the world, giving concerts or spent hours in a recording studio? I couldn't be the kind of friend I was when I got famous and that was clear to me. But I want to change everything. A stupidly nostalgic part of me wants everything to be the way it was, but I don't want that, either. I want everything we had and more."

She looked out the kitchen window and Alice followed the gaze. It was dark out there, of course. Even though the days were supposed to be getting longer, the sun still set before four in the afternoon and didn't rise again until after seven-thirty in the morning.

"Can we talk more tomorrow?" Misty asked, rising from the chair.

"Tomorrow is kind of bad for me. After Liza and I have breakfast and open gifts, we visit my aunts and uncles, cousins – all that family stuff." Alice followed her to the door. "Besides, I'm sure your dad has family who want to see you as well."

"Right. I didn't even think about that. Tomorrow is Christmas day." Leather rustled as Misty thrust her arms into the sleeves of her jacket. She looked lost, which surprised Alice. "What about Monday?"

Alice smiled. "That sounds good. I'll be at work at the Archives. You know where that is. Why don't you come see me in the morning and then I can probably get out at lunchtime for the rest of the day?"

"That sounds like a plan." Misty hesitated by the door, shifting her weight from one foot to the other, and then she leaned forward and brushed a gentle kiss against Alice's cheek. "I'll see you then."

"See you then." Alice held the door open and watched Misty walk to her car. She waited until long after Misty had backed out of the driveway and turned onto the road toward her father's house. With a sigh, Alice leaned her head against the door.

Now that she had unburdened herself – finally let go of her resentment, she wasn't sure she could wait until Monday to see Misty.

But she also wasn't sure she had let go of her fear of Misty leaving her again.

Chapter 10

Misty stood just inside the doorway to the Archives, blinking at her surroundings. When she and Alice were in high school, Alice visited the local libraries whenever she could. Misty had always teased her about wanting to be a librarian, but she thought it was admirable. Whereas Alice could pore over books and manuscripts, get excited about a finding, and chatter on about it, Misty preferred to quietly strum her guitar and create a new tune. They were opposites, opposites who attracted. Alice was simply the one excited by finding information and Misty was the one thrilled by the beauty of song.

Sadly, the thrill was gone. And so was the inspiration.

In their place was money, sure, but there was nothing inspiring about that. Or the fame, the groupies, the corporations courting her for sponsorships...

Misty pushed the thoughts aside as she walked up to the circulation desk. This was the stuff she kept inside – the stuff no one, especially not her manager, knew. This was what she was glad she finally told Alice. Now she hoped she could turn everything around, make it right again. She placed her palms against the surface of the desk and smiled at the pretty blonde girl behind it.

"Hi there," she said. "I'm Misty Morse and I'm looking for Alice Cavanaugh."

"Oh, right! Of course you are!" the girl squealed, holding her hands up to her chin. "Oh my gosh, oh my gosh, oh my gosh!"

This was one of the things that also used to give Misty a thrill – being recognized and gushed over by adoring fans… until they wanted something from her. Something she usually wasn't willing to give.

"I'm sorry for fan-girling, but can I please tell you I have loved your music since I was in junior-high? Your lyrics really speak to the heart, you know? Do you mind if I get your autograph? I hope that's okay with you – Alice told me you would pop in today and I brought your debut CD, if you wouldn't mind signing it."

Misty finally let out a long breath and relaxed. This was the kind of fan she didn't mind so much – one who really listened to her music and wasn't looking for anything more than a smile and a signature. "I'd love to. What's your name?"

"Abigail Fitch. I started at the high school the year after you and Alice graduated, so I never actually got to meet you."

"Oh, you're Deb's little cousin, right?"

"That's right."

"Very cool." Misty wrote out a message on the liner notes with the silver marker she kept in her jacket pocket at all times. Calais was such a small town, considering it was adjacent to the capitol city, and she was glad she remembered Abigail's connection. Then again, she had always been good with names. People liked being recognized and Misty was always happy to make their day. It was a small thing, but important to her and so many others.

Abigail clasped the CD case with both hands as she read Misty's message. "Thank you so much," she said, calmer but still flushed with excitement. "I really appreciate it."

"You're welcome."

"I'll let Alice know you're here." Abigail set the CD on the desk and picked up the phone. "Hey Alice, Misty Morse is here to see you." She nodded and hung up the phone. Before she could say another word, a door behind the circulation desk opened and Alice stepped out of her office.

"Hey, good morning."

Misty felt shy, remembering the kisses they had shared over the last couple of days, especially Christmas Eve. It was the first thing that came to mind as she stood there, looking at Alice. She was also keenly aware of the presence of Abigail, who might not realize her co-worker had such an intimate connection to Misty.

"Cat got your tongue or did you forget how to speak over Christmas?" Alice stared at her for a moment, then rounded the desk and linked their arms together. "Fine, I'll start the tour. Welcome to the Vermont Archives, home of all things Vermont, except maple syrup. However, I'm sure we could find you a history of maple syrup if we look in the right area."

Misty let Alice show her around the Archives, explaining their holdings and tools for research. Even though she wasn't much for libraries, reading, or family history, Misty could see why Alice loved it. There was a huge amount of history contained in the building, going back to pre-Colonial times. Each book, document, or painting Alice pointed out showcased the rich history of the state of Vermont. It was interesting, even for someone who didn't have a deep interest in such things.

There was a brief encounter with Alice's director, who struck Misty as all-business. When the two of them finally entered Alice's office, Misty said, "I can't imagine your sense of humor meshes all that well with your boss's personality."

"Oh, yeah. Well…" Alice leaned over her desk and fiddled with her keyboard. "She's not the warmest person in the world, but she is great at her job. She's actually the one who wanted me to get you in here, not to mention on the podcast. By the way, you don't have to do it, if you don't want to. I know it's not your thing. Abby is excited about it, but we can easily work on another topic for this week's episode if you change your mind."

"Nah, I think it'll be fun. I spent time gathering family stories from Dad yesterday, so I hope I have something interesting to share." It might take her mind off Alice's velvety lips and the curves concealed beneath her dark turtleneck, curves Misty wanted to run her hands along at this very moment.

Alice finished logging out of her computer and picked up her coat. "Well, I'm skipping out of here the rest of the day, so how about lunch? Before you got here, I put together some other things that might be of interest to you."

"Lunch?" Misty slid her gaze toward the door. She really didn't want to encounter another squealing fan today, if she could help it, even if they weren't demanding. When she looked at Alice again, her friend had hesitated, the coat only halfway on her arms.

"Or we can order something and stay here. That works for me." Alice let the coat fall back onto her office chair. "Is that what you'd rather do?"

"Yes, please. This seems like the perfect place to lay low."

"All right." Alice gathered a stack of folders and papers that had been sitting on a corner of her desk and gestured toward the door. "Let's go out into the library itself. I love to work out there. There's a nice, dark, musty corner, perfect for digging up ancestral secrets."

Misty wrinkled her nose. "You and your musty book fetish."

"I know. It's so sexy." Alice winked at her and led her toward the back of the reading area. It wasn't as musty as she made it sound, though, and the atmosphere was definitely conducive to quiet research. "I also took the liberty of drawing up a pedigree chart for you. It covers eight generations, or at least as many as I could get on some of your lines. Some of these names definitely bear further research." Alice removed a rectangle of paper from a manila envelope and unfolded it to reveal the entire chart.

Alice showed Misty one photocopy after another of Morse family historical documents, explaining that they held the originals, which she was also welcome to see. However, some were fragile and these copies were for Misty or her father to keep. She showed Misty how to read the pedigree chart and which people were mentioned in the various documents. After Alice had turned the last page over, she turned to Misty.

"Any questions?"

"Not at the moment. I kind of need to digest all of

171

this, but it's really cool. Like a primer on my family history."

"Yeah, the Morse family was pretty prolific at Maple Corner until not that long ago. Like I said, this is yours to keep. Your dad might want to look through it, too."

"Thanks." Misty gathered the folders and the envelope with the chart, and hugged them loosely. "You know, I never really thought about stuff like this when I was a kid."

Alice let out a chuckle that warmed Misty all over. "I did," she said. "I always wanted to know where I came from. My parents' answers were never good enough for me, because I wanted to know my grandparents' parents, and their parents, and so on. I wanted to know if we had anything crazy in our history, like cattle rustlers or hanging judges. Then I realized I was on the wrong side of the Mississippi to get anything like that."

Now it was Misty's turn to laugh. "Would you really want your claim to fame to be a cattle rustling ancestor?"

"Hey, black sheep ancestors are everyone's favorite. Just look at the genealogical community, especially bloggers. We love digging stuff like that up. It's fascinating to find scandals and know your ancestors did something outrageously unlawful. But it turns out I descend from a large number of Great Migration immigrants – no earth-shattering discoveries there."

"No infamous ancestors for you?"

Shaking her head, Alice traced her fingers along the lines of the heavy wooden table. Misty wished she would trail those fingers elsewhere, like up along her arm, and then draw her into an embrace. When they were teenagers, they used to walk hand in hand and hug often. Even with her apology and Alice's acceptance, it still felt like there was a distance between them.

It's because we hardly know each other anymore. We're both the same as we were then, but… different.

"I do admire the colonists for their courage in crossing a sea to start a new home in an unknown land, of course, but then I think about all the cultural and ethical implications of that. Things like slavery and displacing Native Americans…" Alice sighed and flattened her hands on the surface of the table. "Not every genealogist takes that into consideration when exalting their ancestors' deeds, though, you know? That ticks me off, too. We need to widen the lens through which we look at family history and consider the socio-political ramifications of…"

She stopped and looked at Misty. Then a lopsided grin followed.

"I'm rambling again, aren't I?"

"No, no. It's cute." Misty certainly didn't mind. It was something Alice had done when they were teens – "rambled" about genealogical research and injustice. Of all the things Misty loved about Alice this was, perhaps, the most endearing. She cared, not just about the present, but the past and its impact on the present.

"I'm glad you think so. I feel like I get a little too passionate when I record the podcast or teach workshops."

Better still, Alice was educating others. *Wow.*

Misty smiled at her. Her heart was pounding faster now as she considered reaching out to show some sign of affection – touch Alice's arm, perhaps, or even just nudge her with her elbow. But Misty had never been as physically demonstrative as Alice, so she simply said, "I admire you. You're the real rock star."

"Me? Yeah, right. I don't think giving lectures about why we need to care about how the past affects the present and righting those wrongs makes me a rock star." Alice wrinkled her nose and said, "You're the one who left this town – not that I'd leave it in a million years – but you got out and did something huge with your life."

"I'm just an entertainer, nothing more."

"Are you kidding? Your lyrics touch people's hearts."

Had Alice even listened to her music? Had she kept up with her music career? Misty tilted her head as she wondered.

"But," Alice said, "I have to admit the only time I really listened to your music was when it came on the radio and Liza wanted to hear it. I just couldn't bear to listen on my own. When I heard your first song, I cried. I turned the radio off and then I cried for days." She bowed her head and her shoulders hunched forward.

Misty wanted to ask why, but she waited. Alice would open up without her asking questions. Of the two of them, Alice had never been the one to hold anything back.

"At first, I was excited for you, but after that, I felt awful. You left me for that."

"I know," Misty whispered. As she watched, Alice's shoulders started to shake and she realized her friend was on the verge of tears once more. Hesitantly – reaching out, drawing back, and reaching out again – Misty draped her arm across Alice's back. "I'm sorry for what I did."

She felt Alice's entire body tighten and then relax with a breath. "I know," Alice said, her voice still steady. "I know you are. Just don't do that to me again."

Misty closed her eyes. It hurt to see Alice still in so much pain, but she knew she could allay her fears if only she could find the words. Why was it easier to sing than speak? "Alice, will you go out to dinner with me tonight?"

"Dinner?" Alice looked up at her, eyes wide.

"Dinner, yes, on a date."

"A date with you? A first date?"

"Would it be the first?"

Alice scrunched her nose as she considered the

question. "Technically, yes. Though in the grand scheme of things, not really. Still… Does calling it a date put too much pressure on the whole thing?"

"Maybe, but I want to call it what it is – a woman interested in and attracted to another woman, going to dinner with her, so she can learn more about her."

The light flush that pinked Alice's cheeks surprised Misty. Alice wasn't one to blush. Ever. The color faded a bit as Alice grinned. "Yes, I would love to go on a date with you."

***

It wasn't too difficult to find a quiet, out of the way restaurant where they could have a peaceful dinner. Alice had gone home to change and let Liza know where she would be, and Misty had also gone home to change. It wouldn't do to go on a date in jeans, but what to wear? She had ultimately chosen one of her favorite black dresses and a pair of warm, heavy knit tights. With her boots and leather jacket, she felt comfortable.

Alice was the real stunner, though. When she picked Misty up at her father's house, she hadn't taken off her winter coat when she entered the house and greeted Mr.

Morse. But at the restaurant, she removed the coat to reveal a teal blue shirt with a mandala pattern and black pants that hugged her curves.

She looked so grown-up and Misty wondered how she looked to Alice.

"Wow, it's like you've never changed," Alice said as they sank into their booth and accepted the menus from the server.

They ordered their drinks and an appetizer, and as soon as he walked away, Misty reached up to fiddle with her long, dark ponytail. "Is that a bad thing?"

"Not to me. The look suits you. Why?" Alice flipped through the menu and then looked up at her over it.

"I guess maybe you've grown up quite a bit more than I have."

"Oh, please." Alice snorted and waved her off. "Sure, I had a kid and I had to raise her on my own, but trust me – growing up is a relative term. The big difference between being thirty-eight and eighteen isn't necessarily how we look. It's how we approach the world."

"What do you mean by that?"

Alice set her menu down and folded her hands across it. "When you were eighteen, if you were given a hundred dollars and two options – spend it on a hundred dollars' worth of CDs or pay for something mundane, like an electric bill, what would you do with the money?"

"Back then? Buy the CDs. The electric bill wasn't my problem."

"Right. But nowadays…?"

"Pay the electric bill, because you can't play CDs without electricity."

"Precisely." Alice lifted her menu off the table again. "Maturity is making the rational decisions, rather than the impulsive or self-serving ones, with the knowledge that putting responsibility first means you can play later."

Misty couldn't stop herself from barking out a laugh. "Who are you and what have you done with Alice?"

"I'm Alice from twenty years into the future." Alice winked at her and Misty let out another laugh. This was the way they should be – relaxed and easy together. Able to joke about things.

The server returned with their drinks and they placed their order. After taking a long sip of her soda, Misty said, "I think Liza's a great kid and you're a fantastic mom. It has to be hard, raising her all on your own."

"It is, but even if you raise a child with a partner, you still don't get a manual on child-rearing. It's a learn-as-you-go process. I call her my practice child."

"Are you planning on having more?"

Alice shrugged. "If I do, it certainly won't be the conventional way again. That one night made it very clear to me that I don't lean straight, let alone bi. It also was a very poor substitute for the person I really wanted."

"Me?" Misty whispered.

"Yes, you."

Misty bowed her head as excitement skittered through her. "Alice, I don't want to leave you again."

"I know you don't."

"And I never wanted to stay away so long. But I didn't expect to turn into some kind of huge mega-star. I just thought maybe I'd get a couple albums under my belt and be a musical mid-lister, you know? I never expected the kind of fame I've had."

"And you really don't enjoy it? Not even a teensy bit?"

The sigh Misty released was followed by the confession she knew she had to make. "No. There are certainly honors I've been humbled by, like playing Lilith Fair in '98 and '99. But after that... I don't know. The fame machine churned on and it just wasn't the same."

"What don't you like about it?" Alice asked.

"Everything – the constant madness of going, going, going. The screaming fans. Doing twelve cities in two weeks. It's exhausting. It's grueling. It's not healthy." Misty swirled her drink with her straw. "I'm tired of sucking it up when I have a bad day or I don't feel good, just because the show must go on. I love my music, but when it became work, I started to resent it."

"That sounds awful. Couldn't you get out of it?"

Misty shook her head just as the server returned with their meals. The food smelled so good, Misty couldn't wait to dig into it. "This is another thing," she said, unfurling the cloth napkin from around her utensils. "I miss things like home cooking and small restaurants. Going to the expensive places just to see and be seen never suited me, either. That and fleeing paparazzi. I hate that."

"So if you hated it, why did it go on so long?" Alice twirled her fork in her Fettucine Alfredo and then stuffed the food in her mouth.

"You still eat like a horse, I swear..."

"Mmm," Alice mumbled around the food.

"Yeah, fine then." Misty put a much smaller amount of pasta in her own mouth and swallowed before continuing. Her stomach flipped a bit because she still wasn't accustomed to putting her true feelings and intentions into words. She supposed she would get better with practice and encouragement.

Alice bobbed her head and washed her food down with a drink of soda. "Well, moving on. Keep going."

"Right. Moving on." Misty took a deep breath. "It went on for so long, because I was under contract. My manager, Rick, started me off with that first contract in 1997 and it was pretty short-term. It was for one year. There were extensions after that and more albums, but in

2005, another, bigger label wanted me and they were willing to give me more favorable contract provisions. I accepted in December of that year, but after that, things went in a very different direction."

"Is this a wine conversation?" Alice asked.

"A wine conversation?"

Alice nodded as she waved to the server. "Yeah, the kind that requires some social lubrication."

"No, I think I'm good." Misty felt her breath shudder through her body and wasn't sure if she was telling the truth. All of her TV interviews showed her smiling slightly and saying things like, "I'm so grateful for the opportunity to tour Europe this summer." Where was her cool now, though?

Gone. Evaporated into thin air and all because the truth was coming out of her, one halting sentence at a time.

"Yes, it's a wine conversation," she finally said.

"Great." Alice looked at the server and said, "Could we please get two wineglasses and a bottle of Chardonnay?"

They ate in silence until the server brought the wine

and filled their glasses. Misty took a sip of hers and found that it was the perfect complement to the meal. Still, she wasn't much for drinking, even though it was hard to let out everything she was thinking, so she only took another sip of it before setting it down.

"Why are you so nervous?" Alice asked. "Is this that hard to discuss?"

"I don't know. I mean, yes and no. I feel like some paparazzi is going to jump around the corner at any moment, gleeful that they got a scandalous scoop on me."

"It's all right. Just keep talking."

Misty nodded and tried to regain her train of thought. "So I was under contract and Rick somehow managed to negotiate one long-term. Ten years. I wasn't keen on the idea, but he assured me it was the best contract possible – that it represented security and once it ended, I would have creative control of all my work."

"Wow, that's a long time to have your life controlled by any entity," Alice said. "You should have punched him."

"I should have, but I was exhausted and kind of

jaded at that point. It had been ten years since the start of my career and I felt like I had already lost my best friend, my place in my hometown, and anything else that mattered, so why not just keep doing the one thing I still had?"

"It sounds like I wasn't the only one who had a rough time around that age." Alice's knowing nod reassured Misty. "There's something about being twenty-eight or so that's really difficult. It's like a strange, personal transition point. I don't know how to explain it."

"Saturn return, if you're into astrological explanations," Misty said, a half-smile finally emerging.

"Ha. I'll drink to that." They raised their glasses and clinked them together.

After another sip, Misty continued. "Anyway, I took it at Rick's urging and the label focused on making me bigger. It was heady at first, but then so many new pop stars came on the scene and the label focused on them. There was a huge influx of ingénues they invested in, and I got smaller and smaller shares of attention. It was another turning point for me. I realized at thirty-five or so I was still young and I still wanted to do things; just not the things the label wanted me to do."

The server returned to check on them and Alice requested another basket of breadsticks. As soon as he dropped them off, she said, "So where does that leave you now?"

Misty's heart fluttered. It was time to share the decision she *needed* Alice to give her a reason to make one way or the other.

"My contract ends December 30 and I don't want to sign a new one. My manager came with me on this trip to try to convince me to re-sign, but I came here not to re-sign it. I came here to see if there was another option."

Alice sat perfectly still and for a moment, Misty wondered if she'd heard her. Then she blinked. "You came home to stay?"

"Yes." Misty looked at Alice's hand, the fingers curled loosely around her fork, resting against the table. She wanted to walk her own hand across the table, her fingers lightly skimming the tablecloth, and rest her hand over Alice's.

So she did, a gesture that made Alice blink down at their hands. It was the second time in a single day Misty had taken a chance, had shown affection, had opened herself up to the possibility of either acceptance or rejection.

"But your music…" Alice's chest rose and fell with quicker breaths.

"I don't have the heart to make anything new. Not under my current circumstances. If this continues, there won't be any music. So I've been scouting local real estate and I found a building in downtown Montpelier I could buy that would serve as a recording studio. I've certainly got the money to go indie and maybe even create an indie label to help other locals get their start in music. Not just musicians, of course, but producers and other people interested in working in music."

This time the color that flooded Alice's cheeks was more intense and the smile that followed was radiant. "You want to come back here and stay?" she asked again.

"Yeah, if that's all right with you."

"You don't need my permission to live here."

"Maybe not, but being tired of being a mega-star and wanting to be close to my dad again aren't my only reasons for wanting to come home." Misty's hands tightened over Alice's. "This is where I belong – where I've always belonged."

"That's not true." Alice shook her head and Misty saw wetness shimmering at the corners of her eyes. "You were too exceptional to stay, but I guess you had to go to realize where you wanted to be."

"I wanted to be with you."

Alice let out another snort. "It took you a while to figure it out, I guess."

"I know. Does that mean…" Misty's throat closed up. She had gotten everything else out, but this was the question she was afraid to ask. "Does that mean it's too late?"

"It's never too late when you love someone."

To Misty's surprise, Alice rose, leaned across the table, and brushed a gentle kiss over her lips. She left a lingering taste of Chardonnay and Misty licked at the flavor as Alice sat back down on her side of the booth.

"Don't worry," Alice said. "There's no paparazzi

here. Just a community that's proud of its mega-star, a father who cherishes his daughter, and a woman who would be happy to pick up where the two of us left off all those years ago."

Chapter 11

Alice could not forget the searing good night kiss she and Misty shared after their date. After she got home and got in bed, she stayed awake, replaying it in her mind.

She had pulled up in front of Misty's father's house and put the car in park. All the windows were darkened and the only lights were the front porch and the Christmas tree just beyond the living room window. As she had on Christmas Eve and twenty years before that, Alice initiated the kiss.

When their lips met there in the dark warmth of her car, illuminated only by the distant glow of the colorful lights, Alice wanted to finally take the next step. She wanted to make out as wildly as a teenager, then shove her pants down over her hips and…

Instead she kept her hands locked around her seatbelt as she leaned into Misty, her tongue exploring the open mouth beneath hers. When they parted, Misty's eyes looked glazed-over and Alice knew she could have taken everything further. How long had she denied herself? It certainly hadn't been out of any sense of devotion to

Misty. She hadn't been waiting for her to come back.

It was just that she was busy raising a child and dating was never a big thing for her.

But Liza was well on her way to adulthood and Alice no longer had concerns about what a relationship with another woman might mean to her daughter. Somehow everything was happening now – right time, right place.

Right person?

Alice didn't know and that was the thought that kept her awake.

She said she wants to come home to stay.

Would it work out, though? It seemed easy enough to fall back into being friends, but they had never ventured into being "something more." And what if things got tough – would Misty run again just because of something Alice said or did?

When she finally fell into a fitful sleep, her dreams revolved around their adolescent friendship and that graduation night kiss. Alice wanted to punch her alarm clock when it went off in the morning, since her mind was still lost in the fog of her dreams.

Stumbling from her bed to the bathroom, Alice

showered in the vain hope of clearing the sleep from her mind. By the time she arrived at work, she had already drunk an entire large espresso and felt wired, but not clear-headed.

Abby greeted her with, "Wow, you look awful."

"Thanks, that's always nice to hear." Alice cradled her second espresso in her palms and blinked at Abby.

"I mean…" The blonde glanced at her computer screen and winced. "You've got a class to teach this afternoon. Are you going to be able to teach it?"

"Maybe if I nap, maybe. Or if I don't, maybe that's better. Maybe just more coffee. Maybe."

"Say 'maybe' one more time."

Alice blinked at her blearily. "Why?"

"Nothing." Abby waved her off. "I'll take care of refiling the manuscripts. I suggest you close that door and try to catch up on your sleep."

"Mm, yeah." Alice trudged into her office and closed the door, leaning back against it. It wasn't a bad idea. She could curl up on the rug and take a little nap. Her foggy thoughts cleared just enough to remind her the director was on vacation the rest of the week.

With that, Alice pulled the throw pillow off her chair, tossed it on the floor, set her coffee on the desk, and curled up under her winter coat on the floor.

It felt like hours later when she heard her text notification go off. Sitting upright and feeling better-rested, she rummaged around in her coat pocket for the phone.

Did you have as rough a night as I did?

She grinned. So Misty hadn't slept either? Reaching up to sweep her hair back off her face, Alice pondered her reply. *What are you – psychic?*

After a minute, she received the response. *Maybe.*

Ha, no more maybes.

What?

Alice shook her head. *Joke from earlier. Yes, rough night, but I napped at work. Feeling better.*

Naughty girl?

Sleepy girl. Now wakey girl. Ready for tomorrow night?

It seemed like Misty's next message took forever and Alice finally set the phone on her desk, rose, and took a sip from her espresso. It was cold now and she looked at the clock. Two hours later. She must have really needed the sleep.

Her phone pinged and she scooped it back into her palm.

I am. See you then.

Alice left her office and slipped past the desk to go to the break room. She found Abby at the microwave.

"Oh, I'll just be another minute." Abby looked over her shoulder at her, and then back at the appliance. It dinged and she removed a napkin with a cinnamon roll on it. "Did you get a good nap?" she asked as she stepped aside.

"Yeah. I won't have any problem teaching that class." Alice put the coffee in the microwave and punched in the time she wanted. What she would have a problem with, she realized, was waiting until Wednesday night to see Misty again.

Throughout the day, they exchanged funny, flirty texts. Each message notification sent a little ripple of pleasure through Alice. She left the phone in her office for her class and ran back to it after the last person left the Archives.

Miss you so much. Do we seriously have to wait until tomorrow night?

She blew out a breath as she read and reread the message. Then another dinged through.

Can I sleep over at Tori's house tonight?

Good. The second one meant she could answer the first.

Yes, she texted her daughter, followed by, *Not at all...* to Misty. *Come by around six.*

As soon as she set her phone down, she realized how intensely she wanted to see Misty. Waiting for six tonight might be even more torturous than waiting for Wednesday night. Still, Alice focused on her email, her filing, some research for a client – anything to keep her mind occupied until it was time to close.

Liza had already left for Tori's house when Alice arrived home. She immediately started cooking dinner and then texted Misty, *You can come over any time you want. Hope you-know-what is still your favorite.*

When Misty arrived, Alice hoped she could smell the savory scent wafting through the house.

"You didn't," Misty said, removing her leather jacket

and hanging it on the coat rack by the front door.

"I did."

Misty approached her and slung her arm around her waist. It was all the encouragement Alice needed to go in for the kiss, molding her lips to Misty's hungrily. Misty's other arm went around her waist, her hands locking just above Alice's backside and drawing her flush with Misty's body.

"So you think the way to my heart is through my stomach?" Misty whispered when the kiss ended.

"I think there are many ways to your heart and this is just one of them."

"Mm, meatloaf. That's hot."

"It's not my fault your favorite meal is the least romantic-sounding dinner in the world." Alice grinned and reached up to ruffle Misty's bangs. "These are too long. You should cut them."

"I know I need a haircut and I'll have you know that's not true about the meatloaf. The least romantic-sounding dinner in the world is probably beef stroganoff. It has too many syllables."

Alice chuckled and unwound Misty's arms from her

waist. "So syllables are now a criteria for romance?"

"I'm not sure, but my work is all about putting words to music, so I'm sure I can make sense of this."

"Perhaps." Alice walked to the oven and opened it just enough to let even more of the smell fill the room. The recipe was her mother's and it was one Misty had eaten time and again when they were kids. She loved it so much, she begged Alice's mother for the recipe. Misty's father tried cooking it, but somehow didn't get it quite right.

Alice slipped the oven mitts on her hands and pulled the glass loaf pan out of the oven. "What do you want to drink with it? I've got milk, chocolate milk, soda, beer, water – take your pick."

"Chocolate milk sounds good, like when we were twelve or something."

"I'm not sure if that's a fun idea or kind of skeevy, considering the things I was hoping to do tonight."

There was movement behind her and then Misty's arms went around her waist again. "Oh really?" she whispered in Alice's ear. "You have intentions, eh?"

"I sure do." Alice leaned back against Misty and let

out a low sigh when the other woman's hands moved down the front of her pants.

"As much as I love meatloaf, I think I can wait for it to cool, because I'm very interested in these plans of yours."

"Are you?"

"Mmhmm." Misty nuzzled the side of her neck and Alice felt her knees buckle. She could melt into happiness right now and be done with everything. Here was the woman of her eighteen-year-old dreams, holding her, caressing her, responding to her the way Alice had always wanted.

That graduation night kiss was supposed to lead to mutual confessions of love, not Misty crossing the country without her. Tonight, at long last, Alice wondered if she would be back on track to the love she had craved from Misty for so long.

Misty continued to touch her, those strong hands strumming Alice the way they strummed a guitar. Her fingers moved along the waistband of Alice's pants before unbuttoning them and then pulling down the zipper.

"You aren't going to do this right here, right now," Alice said breathlessly.

"Aren't I? You know me – I don't do anything until someone else makes the first move. You made the moves and now it's my turn." Misty's fingers slid down Alice's pants and curled over her, cupping her through her silky panties. "I have every intention of doing this and then some."

Those fingers continued to rub at Alice, gliding over the fabric with long, firm strokes. Every time the pressure found Alice's sensitive nub, her hips jerked in response. She didn't know how much longer she could hold herself up, but Misty seemed to have everything under control. Her arm encircled Alice firmly, allowing Alice to lean back against her for support.

"You're getting turned on," Misty said, her breath fanning over Alice's ear.

"Of... course... I am." Alice's hips now moved rhythmically, seeking out the caress of Misty's fingers, meeting them eagerly. She felt taut inside – coiled like a spring that was becoming uncomfortably tight. How they had gotten here, Alice suddenly couldn't recall. She just knew it felt long overdue.

"It feels good that you're wet for me. Did you used to feel like this?"

Alice's entire body shuddered with need. "Yes. I would go home and touch myself at night, wanting it to be you."

"Then this is going to feel amazing, since you've waited so long." Misty's hand glided up her panties again, but this time on the downward stroke, it delved below the material and over her heated skin. "Oh yes, you're ready to come, aren't you?"

Reaching back, Alice clung to Misty with both hands. "Y-yes," she stuttered as Misty thrust two fingers inside of her wet passage. She certainly did feel amazing, having Misty touch her like this. The singer's thumb pressed over her clitoris and Alice thought she might die of need as Misty played with her.

"Good," Misty cooed and pressed a kiss against her neck. "Come for me now and I promise to make it worth your while."

Alice let out a sharp gasp as her hips gyrated on Misty's talented hand. Her entire body went weak with ecstasy, a shower of fire sparking over her from head to toe. Even though she lost her ability to stand on her own, Misty cradled her, still thrusting, still circling her thumb, still kissing her neck. Alice felt lost in her embrace, adrift in the warmth and pleasure radiating through her, trusting that Misty wouldn't let her fall.

Misty withdrew her hand and Alice felt her fussing with her pants, pulling them back into place.

"Well then…" Alice finally regained her balance and took a shaky step away from Misty. "I thought dessert was supposed to happen after dinner."

"What's the fun in that?" When Alice turned to Misty, Misty kissed the tip of her nose. "You are so adorable."

"Oh, I bet you say that to all the girls."

"Actually, there haven't been any." Misty stepped aside, so Alice could check the table for plates and utensils.

Alice raised an eyebrow at her. "Really? You must have tons of groupies."

"Sure, and that can be nice, but do you really think I wanted to be with someone who just wanted me for my fame?"

"No," Alice said. "You never were like that. I'm sorry if I doubted you as a person." Her heart was still thumping with exhilaration, but it was slowing now and the ecstatic haze was clearing from her mind.

"Really, I think we keep imagining we've each changed and don't realize that, at our very cores, we're still the same as we were twenty years ago."

Picking up the bottle of dish soap on the side of the sink, Alice said, "Except I am a mom now, so let me be the first to remind you that we should wash our hands before we sit down to the dinner table."

Misty laughed and gently hip-checked her. They both stuck their hands under the stream of warm water Alice started and soon the sink was full of suds. It didn't take long for them to start flicking soap bubbles at each other, but Alice finally turned off the water.

"Keep screwing around and you won't get anything for dinner," she said, tossing a clean dish towel at Misty.

"Withholding Mrs. Cavanaugh's meatloaf would be cruel of you." Misty dried her hands and draped the towel over the oven handle. "You wouldn't lure me here under false pretenses."

"I might. Consider what I've already gotten out of you tonight. Maybe that was my plan all along." Alice snapped her towel in Misty's direction before hanging it alongside the other on the oven.

They sat at the table and soon Alice had their plates heaped with meatloaf, mashed potatoes, and green beans. She watched Misty eat everything on her plate and then go in for seconds.

"And you criticize the way I eat. Doesn't that music money feed you?"

"You'd be surprised." Misty took a drink of water. "I mean, I really don't cook much when I'm home and on the road, it seems like there's no time to eat between shows. Restaurant portions in L.A. are teeny and fancy, not at all filling. Carbs are out. Or maybe its meat that's out. Either way, I didn't realize how hungry I was until you started cooking for me. I've really missed this kind of home cooking."

"What about hiring a maid or a cook?"

Misty shrugged. "I'm not home enough to really justify the expense. That's one of the things I really want to change. As much as I enjoyed the intensity of touring when I was younger, I'd really like to slow things down now. There's just no reason for me to keep up the same, grueling pace. I'm thirty-eight, not twenty anymore. I still want to sing and play guitar, but I want to enjoy my life. I'm tired of being a commercialized human machine."

Alice could only imagine the lifestyle of a rock star and it certainly didn't sound appealing whenever Misty spoke about it. Instead, her voice was laced with regret and frustration when the subject of her work came up, so Alice asked, "Do you remember when you were sixteen and it was all about the love of making music?"

"Hell yeah." Misty's emphatic response told her everything she needed to know. "It feels like… I mean, I don't want to sound like some kind of temperamental or precious artist, or something, but it's as if the purity of what I do is lost in the commercialization of it all."

"That's pretty deep." Resting her elbows on either side of her empty plate, Alice tilted her head and regarded Misty. "So you're really ready to leave it all behind and come back home. Isn't it funny that when you were eighteen, you couldn't wait to spread your wings and fly away from here?"

"Yeah, only to realize the freedom that comes with superstardom is a complete illusion. I'm practically owned by the label and I don't want that anymore." Misty ducked her head. "Those contracts are a bit like indentured servitude. As long as you need the label to market you, all you can do is keep signing on, keep extending the contract. But once you get to the point where you can do your own thing…"

"And you're at that point?"

Misty nodded. "Very much so and I feel better having told you. It's not something I'm exactly advertising, you know? My manager would probably have a hissy fit if he knew I had no intention of signing the new contract."

"Rick? Is he still hounding you?" From everything Misty said about him, Alice couldn't help but imagine he was a rather squirrelly, oily sort of guy.

"Oh, yeah, he still is. Now he's got a new contract he's trying to get me to sign. As if he thinks changing the terms will change my mind." When Misty squirmed a bit in her chair, Alice couldn't help but laugh.

"You really don't want to tell him you don't plan to re-sign, huh?"

"Well, he's been my manager this entire time. I'm his biggest star and I really feel like I'm being disloyal, you know? And I've already had my share of feeling that way about others…"

"Hey." Alice reached across the table and laid her hand over Misty's. "Don't feel that way. Really. Everything with us is in the past. We're moving forward and I'm here for you. I love that even though we've grown up, the old you is still in there." She paused and rolled her eyes. "I don't mean *old* but, well, you know what I'm saying."

Misty chuckled and turned over her hand to gently squeeze Alice's. The warmth of Misty's hand holding hers made Alice shiver with happiness. "I know what you're saying," was the answer.

Their eyes met and Alice took a long breath. "So, Liza is sleeping over at her cousin's house tonight and I was wondering if you wanted to sleep over here…"

Chapter 12

It seemed as though Alice couldn't get her into the bedroom fast enough after her invitation. Every inch of her skin burned as they undressed each other. Misty gathered the bottom of Alice's shirt in her hands and drew it up over her head. Alice was curvy, but fine-boned and petite. It was amazing how much sass that small body contained. Even stripped down to her panties and black lacy demi bra, Alice exuded attitude. She pressed against Misty, claiming her mouth with hungry kisses as she worked Misty's shirt out of the waistband of her jeans.

"I want you," Alice murmured against her mouth. "I always have."

"I know." Misty let Alice remove her shirt and shove her jeans down to her feet. Just as Alice had confessed, Misty had also spent nights alone, thinking of her friend and touching herself. Their sleepovers had been chaste, but fraught with tension she now recognized. Was it possible to have twenty years of pent-up lust? Misty didn't know, but her entire body was afire with the need to find out.

Her heart leapt when Alice threaded her fingers through Misty's hair and pulled her in for another ravenous kiss. *So much strength... Such a tiny body...* Misty's hands dropped to cup Alice's firm backside. She loved dipping her tongue into Alice's welcoming mouth and sliding it over hers. But there were other places she wanted to lick and taste.

Like beneath those silky black panties that she imagined were still wet from her earlier attentions. Was Alice still sensitive from her touch? How would she react when Misty touched her there again?

Even as Misty was considering her actions, Alice was taking action, urging her back toward the bed until they tumbled to the mattress together. Misty loved how Alice always took charge. So many women who had flirted with Misty offered an open invitation and then backed off, expecting her to aggressively take whatever she wanted.

But it wasn't in Misty's nature to pursue. She knew Alice understood that.

And now Alice's hands were drifting down from Misty's hair, along her throat, over her shoulders, and down to her ample breasts. Misty whimpered against Alice's mouth as those soft, small hands circled over her skin, circles that closed in on her nipples without touching them.

"You're an awful tease," Misty told her.

"I know and you love it." The strokes continued – long, lazy ones that left Misty arching toward Alice's hands, yet unable to meet them. Alice had always been accustomed to getting her own way, usually through hardheaded perseverance. If she didn't want Misty to be satisfied, then she would be chasing that satisfaction for a very long time.

"You could be nice to me, you know."

Alice smirked down at her. "I've waited too long to make this easy on you." The smug look on her face sent a thrill through Misty. "You shouldn't have done what you did in the kitchen. Now I can wait a little longer to come again, but it's going to be so much more difficult for you, isn't it?"

Letting out another whimper, Misty wriggled beneath her. Her legs were entwined with Alice's, making it impossible to rub against her. And Alice, that compact force of nature, wasn't giving her any space to maneuver. Even if Misty wanted to try to roll Alice aside, each teasing caress made her weaker and weaker with desire. Everyone mistook her for the tough one – the rock and roll girl who could kick ass and take what she wanted.

But Alice was the one who reached out and took what she wanted with both hands, not Misty. Choices had never come easily to Misty, which was why she had relied upon her manager for so long. Now, though, she was ready to make her own decision and if that meant she could rely on Alice instead, everything would be better.

Alice sat upright, straddling Misty's hips and still fondling her teasingly. "I know how you feel right now," she said. "It's like you just made the most wonderful discovery in the world and can't wait to learn more about it." She finally stroked her thumbs across Misty's nipples, causing her to arch her back and press her breasts into Alice's hands.

"We waited too long," Misty said, biting back a gasp. She had never had such desire burning through her, making her ache for Alice's touch.

"We did and now everything is going to change. Are you ready for that?"

Was she ready? Misty had made so many decisions out of fear. Was she ready to do something she really wanted to do, without worrying about the consequences?

"Yes." She reached up to grasp Alice's upper arms. "I am."

Alice tossed her long, wavy dark hair and nodded. "Then we're going to do this right. No letting the past decide anything anymore. It's you and me, moving forward from now on." She bent and feathered light kisses over Misty's lips, along her throat, then down her chest.

Misty let her arms fall to either side and her head lolled back as Alice devoured her, each kiss scorching a path across her skin. Where Misty was night, Alice was day – intense and unrelenting. Both fear and elation mingled inside Misty, heightened by Alice's dizzying kisses. Misty thought she would lose her mind when Alice's lips finally closed around one of her nipples, her tongue making long, slow passes over the bud of flesh.

If she felt this ecstatic now, what would happen when Alice's touch moved lower, her lips seeking out even more intimate areas? The very thought sent a jolt through Misty and she moaned with anticipation. She didn't know if she could handle more than this.

Alice's mouth moved to her other breast, repeating the same torturous licks. The dull, throbbing ache between Misty's thighs dominated her thoughts. She desperately needed to spread her legs, to alleviate the sensation. Having them pressed together by Alice's knees on either side of her only made it worse.

The kisses moved even lower, trailing over and across her stomach, followed by Alice's hands. Those hands passed over Misty's hips to rest on top of her thighs. "You look so sexy right now," Alice said. "Like I've never seen you before."

"Desperate?" Misty asked, lifting her head.

"A little bit. It's adorable." Alice rubbed her hands along Misty's thighs, moving her fingers inward as she did so. "I know you want me right here, making love to you, fucking you – whatever you need at this very moment."

"All of it. I need all of it."

Alice let out a low laugh. "I'll see what I can do." Her hands finally entered the space between Misty's thighs and urged them apart. Misty obliged Alice, her legs falling open and inviting her to do whatever she wanted there.

If she hoped for any kind of relief, though, she was denied it. Alice didn't do anything but look for the moment, her hands still caressing the insides of Misty's thighs, sending little electric shocks through her body. Misty wondered what Alice was thinking as she knelt between her thighs, her gaze intent.

Then she felt Alice's hands make their way up her thighs, to the juncture of her womanhood. Those searching fingers framed her opening and then she felt Alice's breath fan over her flesh – a tease of things to come. Misty couldn't help but lift her hips, beckoning with them.

The flat of Alice's tongue against her was the most surprising sensation of all. Misty thought she would draw out the teasing yet, but no. With one long, leisurely lick, Alice had her twisting on the bed, gasping with pleasure. Each lick that followed was sweeter than the first, until it seemed the time between them blurred into one continuous motion – Alice lapping at her relentlessly and Misty feeling completely lost on waves of bliss.

Her hands clutched at the blankets. She was so sure this was the moment, the release she was waiting for...

"I don't think so."

Misty blinked as she tried to process Alice's words.

"It takes two to tango and I plan to participate in the dance; not just lead."

Thoughts were hazy as Misty tried to understand the analogy. Why would Alice pull out one of her mind-boggling word games now, of all times?

And then as Alice's knees settled on either side of Misty's head, she understood. That bare, glistening blossom that lowered toward her face and then hovered just over her mouth – that was what she needed to think about now.

Misty brought up her arms to wrap them around Alice's hips and pull her down over her face. The scent that filled her senses was earthy and sensual – one she had always appreciated. Misty opened her mouth and took her first taste of Alice.

Like honey.

That was the initial thought that came to mind when her tongue met that supple, ready flesh. Somehow, she forgot for a moment that she was receiving the same pleasure and lost herself in Alice's offering. Alice settled atop her and Misty feasted on her, first running her tongue along that drenched seam and gathering the juices there. She felt Alice's head between her thighs, the mouth over her own aching pussy, the tongue swirling around her clitoris.

She was back on the edge of bliss, so close to losing control. Misty couldn't go it alone, she decided, so she latched onto Alice's clitoris and suckled at it relentlessly. Above her, Alice's body quivered and her thighs tensed. Misty felt Alice mirror her actions, sucking on her until her hips also jolted in response.

Rapture lashed at her and there was no controlling her orgasm now. All she could do was bury her face between Alice's thighs, sucking and licking at her mindlessly as her body rode the sensation. Alice bucked against her face and they both clung to one another, compelling one another to mutual pleasure until Misty threw her head back and gasped for breath. She felt Alice do the same, her body giving one more shudder before relaxing on top of her.

"Holy shit," Alice panted, rolling to her side. "Holy… shit."

Misty pressed her hands to her heaving chest and couldn't stop the giggle that mingled with her breaths. "You said it."

"That was…" Alice sat up and raked her hair back away from her face. "That was fucking amazing."

"And why did we wait so long to act on our feelings?"

"No, no. None of that. Remember what I said." Alice turned and pushed the comforter away from the pillows. "Get under here with me," she demanded.

Misty did and soon she was under the blankets, and in Alice's arms. "That was just the best. Ever."

"I know." Alice draped her leg over Misty's legs and nuzzled the back of her neck. It felt wonderful to be cuddled and loved, and Misty closed her eyes as she savored the sensations still rippling through her.

"I've never felt so happy."

"Not even on stage or when you signed your first record deal or something?"

"Uh-uh." Misty wriggled until she felt their bodies mold together perfectly. "I've always needed you there with me. Success is empty if you don't have anyone to share it with."

Alice pressed a kiss to her cheek. "Ancient history now."

"Yes. I'm ready to move forward. If you want me here, I'm here."

"I've never not wanted you here."

Blinking, Misty opened her eyes again. Tears burned at the corners of them and she felt her nose stuff up in response. "Really?"

"How many times do I have to say that's in the past? We talked about it. We both made mistakes. We're here now and that's what matters."

"Mmkay…" Misty felt drowsy and her eyes fluttered shut, effectively stopping the tears. She sniffled once and her breathing evened. "I can do anything as long as I have you," she said. "Anything."

"No, you don't need me to be able to do anything, but it sure is nice to know someone else has your back." Alice's arms tightened around her. It felt so nice to be held as she drifted off to sleep, and that was the last conscious thought Misty had.

Chapter 13

Alice looked over the list of questions Abby had put together for the podcast and shook her head. "This is all so generic. I don't think we should treat this like our usual interview," she said.

"You don't?" Abby stood in her kitchen, stirring cocoa into a cup of hot milk.

"No way. Remember, we're not interviewing our usual genealogist or historian. This is a local celebrity and do you really think the question about what got her into genealogy is even pertinent? Instead, this should be more about Misty's stories about Maple Corner and Calais, and what it was like to grow up in the Morse family. We shouldn't be professionally focused." Alice rose from the table and got a mug out of the cupboard for herself.

She had left a sleeping Misty in her bed when she went to work that morning and spent the entire day eager to see her again. Misty had gone home not long after, texting Alice to let her know she left the door unlocked for Liza.

Now it was almost seven o'clock in the evening, the

time Alice and Abby always broadcast and recorded
Mom Genes, which meant Misty would show up any –

The doorbell rang and Liza ran from the hall to the
living room yelling, "I'll get it!"

"Wow, she's fast," Abby observed.

"Blame me. I haven't given her a chance to drool
over her musical idol this week."

"Really? You ought to let those two hang out,
considering Liza wants to be a producer. I'm sure the kid
wants to ask Misty a zillion questions."

Alice got her mug of water out of the microwave as
it dinged. Dropping a sachet of green tea into the cup,
she nodded. "You're right. Maybe I need to invite Misty
to hang out after the podcast, so Liza can drive her away
with questions."

"I don't know." Abby shrugged and gave her a half-
smile. "I don't get the impression that Misty is someone
easily driven away."

*Except when she's not sure how to handle
complicated emotions.*

Alice winced. Where had that thought come from?
After all, she had been the one advocating leaving

everything in the past, right?

Misty waved as she walked into the kitchen, Liza trailing along behind her like a shadow. "So is this where the magic happens?"

"No, we're going to my office." Alice glanced at Liza, who was furrowing and unfurrowing her brow, and jerking her head toward Misty. "Since the podcast is only an hour long, maybe you'd like to stick around and hang out afterward," Alice offered, looking at Misty again. "I know Liza has been dying to chat with you."

"Sure, I'd love that."

Alice saw Liza thrust her fists in the air and do a victory dance behind Misty.

"Great. And you remember Abby, of course."

"I do." Misty smiled and Alice was surprised to see Abby turn at least three shades of red. She hadn't been fazed to see a teenager like Tori star struck, but a rational, reasonable adult? Maybe they saw something Alice didn't, because as far as she was concerned, Misty was... Misty.

Except Alice's heartbeat quickened when she looked at Misty again. Sure, she might have been Misty, but now she was Alice's Misty.

She cleared her throat and gestured toward the hall. "This way, then, ladies." The office was just another bedroom, not as large as the other two, but large enough to accommodate a desk, small set of bookshelves, and a loveseat.

Alice sat at the desk and set up the podcast software and connection, while Misty and Abby sat on the sofa. Liza leaned against the doorframe, arms folded. "Do you mind if I stay?" she asked plaintively.

"Only if you promise not to derail the conversation," Alice said. "No squealing, no fangirling, and try to keep any questions or contributions on topic."

"If you don't mind," Misty interjected, "could you give me an idea of what kinds of questions you're asking?"

"I want to avoid any sort of script, actually. Instead, I'd rather treat this like a conversation about your memories of growing up here and memories about things or family stories of historic or genealogical significance. Will that work for you?"

Misty nodded and leaned forward, her elbows

propped on her knees and her hands clasped. "Yes."

"Great. Do you want anything to drink before we start?"

"Just water."

"I'll get it." Liza spun from the doorway and dashed toward the kitchen.

Clicking on her mouse, Alice said, "We're starting, then. Abby and I will do our intro and then introduce you. Does that sound good?"

"Oh yeah, it sounds just like radio and television, only better because it's with friends."

Alice wasn't sure if Misty was teasing her or not, but the wink her friend threw her way allayed her concerns. She pressed the button that would put them live on the air and played the intro music. As soon as the fifteen seconds of sound were done, she said, "Good evening and welcome to another episode of *Mom Genes*. I'm Alice."

"And I'm Abby," her co-host chimed in, "and we're your friendly local genealogical information specialists."

"Today's show is going to be fun for all ages."

Abigail grinned as she relaxed and found her groove. As

223

with teaching, she loved to speak in front of others, even if they were on the other side of a computer. "This month, Union 32 High School's class of 1996 celebrated its twentieth reunion and guess what? If you're a Gen Xer who went to our school, you're probably familiar with our guest. You might have even been in a class or two with her."

Misty chuckled and said, "Just don't blame me if I don't remember those classes."

"Oh, come on now, Misty. Is that any sort of example to set for the kids at the high school now who worship the ground you walk on?" Alice was so glad Misty fell easily into witty banter with her. Of course, she loved doing the show every week, but this was the first time she had a guest who was not a genealogist or historian.

"Classes are important, but, you know, stuff and things about academics and whatnot."

Alice laughed and Abby said, "Words of wisdom from Calais' own superstar."

"Well, since your impressive musical career is common knowledge, let's get right to the point – is this

kind of talent the norm for the Morse family, Misty?"
Alice asked.

"That's a good question." Misty tilted her head as
she considered it. "First of all, I have to admit I knew
nothing about my ancestry until you took the time to
give me a tour of the Archives and show me some really
cool documents about my family. My dad, well, I think
he's talented just because he put up with me. I know I
wasn't the most difficult teenager, but I still wouldn't
wish a daughter on a single father. It's so unfair."

To Alice's delight, the conversation flowed well
between all three of them. Liza seemed perfectly content
to sit on the floor and listen. The episode ran longer than
most and the podcast's Facebook page was more active
than ever with questions and comments from listeners.

Almost an hour into the conversation, Alice said,
"Now that we've talked a little bit about Morse family
history, let's check out some of these Facebook
questions. Oh no, Deb Fitch wants to know if we
remember the first time we ever walked into the
Whammy Bar." Alice shook her head. "Deb, we were
too young to be there, you know, but they let us hang out

and order food anyway."

"Hence the whole 'Whammy Bar Kids' thing," Misty added. "But, really, I've got a question for Deb – what's this I hear about the Fitches out-populating the Morses in Maple Corner? Something about an evil intermarriage plot between Fitch men and Morse women."

Abby covered her mouth with her hands. Her eyes were already overflowing with tears of laughter.

"Well, Deb just posted 'Them's fightin' words,' Misty, so I think you better back off of that subject." Alice knew she could use it as a way to get the episode back on track. "Of course, back when Maple Corner first existed, the Morses were one of the first and most prolific families in that area of Calais. To this day, this remains one of the smallest and closest-knit communities on the very border of a capitol city. That's one of the things I love about our town."

"Me too," Misty agreed, "which is why it was so great to come home for the reunion and get an education about my ancestry. I appreciate it more than you both know, and so does my dad."

"That's what we're here to do." Alice opened her mouth to say more, but her chest seemed to fill with pressure. It was overwhelming, not allowing her to speak or breathe as she looked across the room at Misty and realized...

I love her.

Somehow Abby picked up the slack and filled the silent void. Alice barely registered her words, because her own thoughts were colliding in her mind.

It's not like when I was sixteen and realized I was in love with her. It's totally different now. The same, but different. It never went away – it just changed.

Now Abby and Misty were laughing at something Misty said. "I think plenty of listeners will remember your grandfather doing that." Abby chortled and wiped tears away from her eyes. "Well, I think that's all the time we have for tonight, right Alice?"

"Right." Alice straightened in her chair and turned to her computer. They were just over an hour. How had the time gone by that quickly? Even though she fumbled over her words, she rattled off their usual sign-off, including a plug for next week's guest, a local geneablogger. As soon as she signed out of the recording software, she let out a heavy sigh.

Getting distracted was so unlike her, but Misty had been nothing but one heck of a week-long distraction, first a negative one and now one she couldn't get enough of.

Well, hell. She had it and she had it bad.

Abby, Misty, and Liza were now having a lively conversation behind her, while she responded to Facebook comments and finalized the podcast file. As soon as it was saved and uploaded to various sites, she put the computer to sleep and turned to the women behind her.

"I better get going," Abby said, rising from the sofa. "Work tomorrow, you know. Thanks for being on the show, Misty. I think people are going to love it."

"We got a great response from our Facebook listeners," Alice added with a grin. "I'm sure with the name 'Misty Morse' as one of our keywords, we'll get more hits and downloads than ever."

"Oh, I see." Misty also stood and hooked her thumbs in her belt loops. "Using me for my fame. Nice, Alice.

Real nice." She was smiling, though, actually grinning from ear to ear.

They wandered into the kitchen, where Abby said her goodbyes and left. Alice stretched her arms out to her sides and gathered her hair to pull it back off her shoulders. "That was probably the strangest episode we ever recorded, but I think it was the most fun, too."

"I had fun. It was more relaxed than my usual interviews." Misty leaned against the counter, arms folded. "It felt good to talk without having to market some new album or tour." There was a low buzz and she reached into her jeans pocket to pull out her cell phone. Her brow furrowed as she glared at the phone, but then smoothed out when she stuffed it back into her pocket. "Hey, Liza, I was thinking – do you want to go out to lunch with me tomorrow?"

"Me?" Liza squeaked, bringing her clenched fists to her mouth and her eyes going wide.

"Yes, you. I know you want to talk about producing music and I'd be happy to answer your questions, if I can." Misty looked at Alice. "What do you think?"

Alice felt that pressure fill her once more. Her best

friend – lover, now? – wanted to spend quality time with her daughter. "That sounds wonderful to me," she said when she recovered her voice. "I would appreciate it as much as Liza if you're willing to take the time to do that."

"Great and maybe we can get together tomorrow night after you're off work. But this time let dinner be my treat, will you? I'll bring something here." Misty looked so earnest and eager, that Alice wanted to kiss her then and there. But she refrained, instead picking at the dishtowel hanging on the oven handle.

"Oh yes, Mom, that would be so cool, wouldn't it?" Liza asked, jumping up and down.

"Very cool." Alice smiled. Unlike so many single moms, she certainly hadn't wanted to find a father-figure for her child. So the fact that Misty was genuinely interested in helping Liza learn more about something she was passionate about made her feel all kinds of sappy. She didn't want to jump the gun, but she realized she should explain her relationship with Misty to Liza before it came out in some other way.

Misty seemed to pick up on Alice's thoughts,

because she gave a nonchalant shrug and said. "I better get going. I'll be here tomorrow to pick you up at eleven-thirty, Liza." With a little wave, she turned toward the door.

Alice scurried after her, catching up just as Misty plucked her leather jacket down from the coat rack and opened the front door. "Hey," she whispered, "what about…"

"Us?" Misty turned and raked her gaze along Alice's body as she shrugged into her jacket, before looking back up at her face. "I'm sure you want to talk to your daughter about us before it goes any further, but I foresee a whole lot of 'us' being a thing if you're still in."

"Oh yes, I am all kinds of in."

"Good." Misty kissed her on the cheek and stepped out into the cold night. Alice watched until Misty pulled out of the driveway, then turned to see Liza standing in the living room, arms folded and gaze expectant.

"We still have to talk about what happened between you two," Liza said. "You've owed me since before Christmas."

Alice shut the door behind her and locked it. "Yeah, we do. I suppose 'it's complicated' isn't enough of an explanation for you."

"Nope. Come on, mom."

"Right." Alice stepped into the living room and flopped down onto the couch. Liza chose the other end and watched her. Alice prefaced her explanation with, "So you saw the photos of me and Misty in the yearbook."

"Yup, and I found out around town that you two were best friends. Totally inseparable in the 80s and 90s. So what happened?"

Alice did her best to recount the past sensitively, but without withholding any information. It felt strange to tell her daughter about the kiss, especially since she had never shared it with any of her adult friends, except Deb and Derek, and then how she felt when Misty told her she was going to Seattle alone.

"Wait, mom, we covered the whole gay thing when I was, like, five, but did your friends know?"

"Oh, yes. Definitely. It's not like I run around screaming 'look at me, I'm a huuuge lesbian,' but Deb and Derek, and everyone I've hung out with for years knows. But only a few people know about the Misty kiss." Alice nodded and continued. "I don't think it was quite as obvious when I was younger, because I was still figuring it out for certain. But after the night that gave me the most fantastic thing in my life –" she pointed at Liza "– I knew without a doubt that I was gay and I didn't feel the need to hide it."

"Were you always in love with Misty?"

Alice thought about the question. "Pretty much. I think I became far more aware of it when I was about sixteen and that's how it stayed. And I guess you should know that Misty and I have cleared up our past issues and, well, we've been on a couple of dates."

A long moment of silence stretched between them and Alice waited for Liza to react. She knew it wouldn't be a negative reaction, but she couldn't gauge exactly what it *would* be.

"Wow," Liza finally said. "That is so cool. My mom is dating a celebrity and that celebrity… Holy crap, she could become my other mom!"

"Now, don't go that far."

"But mom, that would the coolest thing ever! Imagine if I could go back to school in January telling everyone Misty is my other mom!"

"No, no, no." Alice held up her index finger. "First of all, Misty and I are still getting to know each other again. We're just dating and doing all the things that people who are dating do. That doesn't mean we're moving in or getting married."

"Yet."

"Fine. Yet. Possibly never, though, so please don't get so excited. Misty and I are just two adults with a shared past who finally have the chance to maybe share our future."

Liza nodded, her brows lowered, her gaze serious. "So does that mean we're moving to L.A.?"

"Oh jeez." Alice slapped her hand over her forehead. "Okay, that's another thing I want to talk to you about. Misty has entrusted me with some very personal information and she may do the same with you tomorrow. I'm not entirely sure, but I want you to promise me that whatever she tells you is between the two of you. Do you understand me?"

Alice could count on one hand the number of times she had ever scolded Liza. It wasn't something she liked doing and it usually wasn't necessary, but she wasn't about to have her daughter jeopardize Misty's career.

"Yes, I understand. You know me, Mom." Liza's delicate features softened and Alice leaned across the couch to hug her.

"Thank you, honey. Please understand I do trust you and I want Misty to trust you, too. She's just in a place where she's making some very big decisions right now and I want you to keep that to yourself if she talks to you about it, okay?"

Her daughter's slim arms wrapped around her in a tight hug. "Okay, Mom."

Alice kissed Liza's forehead and smiled. "I'm really proud of you, you know. You're smart, you're feisty, and you're sensitive. Thanks for being you."

"Aw, don't let having a girlfriend turn you all sappy, Mom."

Chapter 14

Misty stood backstage, grinning. She realized she'd been grinning for at least four days, ever since her Tuesday night date with Alice. Wednesday night doing the podcast with Alice. Thursday at lunch with Liza and then dinner with the both of them. Alice had asked her to stay over and Liza had conveniently gone into her own bedroom, turned up her radio, and given them what she unashamedly called "alone time." And then they spent all of Friday together, going through old photos, both of them and Liza from her infancy.

As far as Misty's relationship with Alice was concerned, she knew the jig was up. Three dates. Sex on the second date. An accepting daughter who had walked into lunch armed with not just questions about the music industry, but excitement about their relationship.

Alice Cavanaugh is my girlfriend.

Nothing could be better. Nothing.

The high school auditorium was pretty much exactly like Misty remembered it, except with updated technology. When she first arrived in the quiet, almost-empty school late in the afternoon, she had wandered the halls with Deb Fitch, reminiscing about their days as students there.

"I can't believe you decided to be a teacher," Misty told her.

Deb had laughed and shrugged. "I never want to leave this place. It keeps me young."

After that, Misty had stood at the center of the stage, looking out at the auditorium. Soon the school would fill up with young New Year's Eve revelers, all eager to see a concert by their famous "native daughter."

But for the moment, Misty savored her memories of talent shows and theatrical productions, of standing center stage, strumming her guitar, and singing. Initially, she had started with covers of songs, especially early Joan Jett. There was even the year she cut off her hair just so she could look like Joan.

She had spent her summer between sophomore and junior years writing her own songs, while Alice was at her side, usually immersed in some history book or fiddling with her family tree. Alice had always been her first audience, hearing each song as Misty composed it and then the final product when it was woven together as a complete piece, accompanied by her guitar.

Alice had been her first true fan, unwavering, always supportive... and always telling the truth, even when it hurt.

Misty knew now that Alice's honesty had not been a bad thing. It had been what she needed to hear, to know even the girl who loved her didn't think she was perfect or could do no wrong. Better to hear it from someone who cared, though, and who gave her honest opinion out of a desire to help her do better, than to hear it from someone who just wanted to drag her down.

Now she wanted to tell the world what Alice meant to her.

But she knew she had to take it one step at a time. First of all, she was still a huge star with her record label and under a ridiculous amount of pressure to extend the contract that had expired yesterday. Rick still called, texted, and emailed her constantly from L.A. with updates about the contract, concessions the label was making in the hope of keeping her signed.

But you're really pushing it. They're getting

impatient, had been his last message.

So what. They could get impatient.

Misty tossed her too-long bangs and smoothed her ponytail. There was something more important than making the label happy.

Making herself happy.

She looked up as Deb strolled backstage with a couple of tall young men. "James and Gavin usually work backstage for our theater productions," she told Misty. "So they'll help out tonight with the curtain and anything else back here. Boys, this is Misty Morse."

"Hi, guys." Misty shook their hands. Neither of them looked particularly impressed, which was a relief. It was usually the girls and women who lined up, squealing with excitement, outside the venues she played, anyway.

"Other faculty members should be arriving shortly and getting students situated, so I think all you have to do is, well…" Deb shrugged. "Whatever you do before a show. Is there anything I can get you?"

"Nah, I'm pretty low maintenance. I don't demand green M&Ms or cocaine."

"Well, that's good, because I'm all out of M&Ms

and I'm not sure I want to share my coke."

"Ms. Fitch," one of the boys – Misty remembered he was Gavin – said and shook his head.

Deb rolled her eyes. "Kids today. Boys, this is what adults call a joke. From time to time, we say untrue things that we think are funny. That doesn't make it right, though, so remember that."

As Deb walked away with the teenagers, Misty smiled. It looked like this was the right choice for Deb after all. When they were teenagers themselves, they had hopes and dreams, goals and ambitions. It looked like Deb, Derek, Alice, and Misty had achieved them. She still wasn't completely sure about Nick, since he had never talked about any particular career goals. But if he was happy doing what he was doing, then she was happy for him.

Rather than continue mulling over her thoughts, Misty sat down on the stool they had set behind the curtain for her and strummed her guitar. She practiced a few chords and then stepped out on stage to do the same. As she played, she got a feel for the auditorium again and modulated her volume accordingly. She sang the chorus of one of her favorite songs, experimenting with the sound. When the last note faded to silence, she heard footfalls outside the auditorium doors. People were coming.

She stepped back behind the heavy curtains and set her guitar next to the stool. When she looked up, Liza and Alice were standing in the wings at stage right, waving at her.

"Friends." She wrapped one arm around each of them before they could react. "I'm so glad you're here!"

"We wouldn't miss it for the world," Alice said, returning the hug. She smelled of cinnamon and Misty couldn't help but sniff at her neck. "Stop that. I baked Snickerdoodles after dinner. Come on by and you can have as many as you want."

"That's funny, considering you wanted to avoid Misty when you first found out she was coming." Deb walked by, shaking her head. "Now look at you two. It's about damn time."

Misty felt Alice stiffen in her hug, but she just laughed. "If you were trying to avoid me, you've done a really bad job of it." She stepped back and smiled at them. "Do you want to watch from back here?"

"No thanks." Liza shook her head. "We got Tori to save us seats in the fourth row, center. Best place to watch. Break a leg."

Alice frowned at her, but Liza just took her by the hand and led her offstage, muttering, "That's showbiz speak, Mom. Don't you know anything?"

The hum beyond the closed curtain swelled and Misty knew the auditorium was getting full. She certainly didn't need Deb to walk up to her and say, "It's a packed house out there." No. Misty knew the sound of a full house, one buzzing with anticipation.

She had started in smaller venues than this and progressed to immense stadiums. Now she knew how much she missed those small stages, where she felt like she could make a stronger connection with her audience. Where she wasn't a tiny dot to the tens of thousands of people seated around the stage. Where she didn't have to rely on a seven-story tall television screen to allow her fans to actually see her.

One of the boys, James, scampered behind her, picked up the stool, and carried it out onto the stage. The audience whistled and cheered as he did so. Before Misty could wonder if they would be kept waiting, she heard Deb's voice reverberating through the auditorium.

"I know everyone is excited about our special guest, who was gracious enough to agree to give a New Year's Eve concert just for our very own students. So please welcome home, from the Union 32 class of 1996, Misty Morse!"

The curtain opened just enough for Misty to walk on stage, her guitar in her left hand so she could wave with her right. She approached the microphone, settled the guitar strap over her shoulder, and closed her eyes.

As soon as her fingers found the chord she wanted, she opened her mouth and the song emerged. It was nostalgic for her, because it was the first radio single she had ever recorded. It was the last song she had ever sung for Alice, because it was the first one Alice had ever criticized.

Alice's critique had been right, though. Misty knew that now, because both Rick and her producer at the time had helped her shape the song into something truly beautiful. It was still raw and not nearly as mature as her later work, but at the time that had captured the attention of the first label to pursue her.

She opened her eyes and looked out over the crowd. The lights weren't as blinding as she was accustomed to and she could see every face looking at her, every student and adult watching her with shining eyes.

When the song ended, the auditorium exploded into applause, which brought tears to Misty's eyes. She leaned close to the microphone and said, "Hey there, Calais. It's been too long." A fresh round of applause filled the room and she waited until it quieted. "I don't know about you guys, but I'm really excited about 2017 and nothing could be more special than seeing in the New Year with all of you."

Stepping back from the mic, Misty launched into her next song. As she surveyed the room, she found both Alice and Liza in the fourth row, Liza and Tori bobbing their heads to the music. To her delight, her father was there, sitting next to Alice and beaming with pride.

And Alice? Alice just looked overjoyed as she finally listened to Misty's music.

Yes, her dreams had been worth following and

despite the pain – or maybe because of it – coming home to the people she loved was the payoff.

As soon as the concert concluded and Misty led the countdown to the New Year, she slipped backstage and dabbed the sweat off her forehead with the towel James handed her. "Thanks," she said when he offered her a bottle of water. He had been as efficient as any roadie, offering hydration as she sang, dealing with any small technical issues, and even swapping out the stool when she wanted something a little more comfortable. Gavin must have remained behind the scenes, working the curtain rigging and lighting, because she didn't see him again all night.

Or, no, it was morning now. January 1, 2017. A whole new year and, if she could only find the courage to put her foot down with her manager, a whole new life for her. She put her guitar in its case and latched it. For a moment, she remained in a crouch, considering her next course of action.

"Hey, Misty?"

She looked up to see Deb standing a few feet away

from her. Unfolding herself, Misty smiled. "What's up?"

"If you're up for it, I know the kids would love to get autographs and photos with you."

"Absolutely." She followed Deb offstage and into the gymnasium, where the faculty had set up refreshments for everyone. For the next hour, Misty took photos with the kids and their parents, signed CDs, and chatted with the teachers.

The crowd trickled out leaving only a handful of people by one in the morning. Misty knew at some point before then, her father had gone home, but she was pleased to see that Liza and Alice were still there, chatting with Deb and helping her clean up the gym.

She ambled over to them and said, "Hey, friends."

"That was fantastic," Liza enthused. "We loved it, but you don't need me to tell you that." She picked up a bag full of trash, tied it, and slung it over her shoulder.

Misty watched as she crossed the gym. "Wow, she really is a cool kid. It's nice of her to help."

"I think she's looking to get some brownie points." Deb shrugged and finished clearing off the table, swiping the paper tablecloth and remnants of half-eaten snacks into a trash can. Misty glanced at Alice, who remained quiet. Was she in the same contemplative mood as Misty?

Rather than wait to find out, she walked up to Alice, framed her face between her hands, and kissed her gently. Alice responded by placing her hands on Misty's hips and teasing her with the very tip of her tongue. When they parted, Misty heard someone whistle.

"Again, it's about damn time." Deb raised her hands and clapped, shaking her head. "Seriously. I thought you two would never get together."

"Shut up," Alice muttered, ducking her head.

"Alice, at a loss for words? Now that's a first."

Misty turned to face Deb, but kept her arm draped across Alice's shoulders. "I'd like to think I can take some credit for that," she said with a half-smile.

"Well, I'm sure everyone is tired and wants to get home. Go on. The custodians and I have got this."

"Are you sure?" Liza asked, bouncing back to stand next to Misty and Alice.

"I'm sure. Go on and enjoy your last day of freedom before school starts on Monday."

"Oh no, back to school already?" Liza's whine belayed her previous excitement and she drooped. "Well, then, I guess we better go. Good night, Deb. Um, I mean Ms. Fitch."

They turned to walk out of the building together and Misty hesitated at the doors. "Do you want to go home and get your sleep?"

Alice shook her head and nuzzled against her neck. "The last thing I want right now is sleep. I think I'm still a little wired. Why don't you spend the night at my place?"

Misty's fingers closed around the cellphone in her pocket. It vibrated with a reminder she had set. A reminder that her return flight to L.A. was, like the resumption of the school year, on Monday morning.

"Let me get my guitar from backstage and then I'll come over," she said. Like magic, however, the moment the words left her mouth, James was at her side with the guitar case and leather jacket. Misty chuckled, took her jacket, and put it on. "Or not. Thanks, James. You rock."

"No," he said, "you do. Thanks for the concert. It was great." He glanced at Liza and said, "I'll see you tomorrow."

"Sure." She watched as he walked away, her head turning as if it were on a swivel.

Alice and Misty followed her gaze. "I thought there was no one in this town worth dating, according to you," Alice said.

"Um... Hey, look – it's snowing." Liza pointed toward the doors and they looked outside at the softly falling flakes.

Misty watched them drift to the ground, the snow sifting into crevices and settling over surfaces, and smiled. Could the start to the New Year be any more perfect than this?

Chapter 15

Back at the house, Alice watched Liza trudge to bed, rubbing at her eyes and mumbling about how unfair it was that winter break was nearly gone. Alice felt the same way and she turned to Misty.

"We need to talk about what happens next." She hated to end a wonderful evening like this, but as she hung up her coat and scarf, she knew it was a conversation that had to happen.

Misty hung her jacket on the rack and nodded. "I have a round trip ticket. I'm supposed to fly back to L.A. on Monday."

Well, shit.

"But it's only going to be temporary."

"It is?" Alice thrust her hands in the back pockets of her jeans and watched Misty expectantly.

"Yeah. After tonight – after the whole week, but especially tonight – I can't go on like this. I know that for certain now." Misty held her hands up as if that would help her find the words she needed. "No stadium concert ever felt as good as coming here and playing for people who know me, who are proud of me for becoming something, you know? I want to do that and I want to do colleges and coffeehouses again. Not become some sort of has-been, but transition into indie music. I'm so tired of trying to be marketable. I want to sing the songs that are inside of me."

It was the longest speech Alice had heard Misty make since high school, when she once scolded their group of friends about how selling out was the worst thing anyone could do.

Almost as if she were channeling that memory of her eighteen-year-old self, Misty said, "I became the thing I didn't want to be. Sometimes it was worth it but, more often than not, it wasn't."

"So. Monday." Alice pursed her lips as she twisted her body back and forth, her hands still jammed in her back pockets as if that was the only thing holding her upright. "Monday you're leaving."

"But I'll be coming back as soon as I can."

"What do you have to do out there?"

Misty looked up at the ceiling. "Jeez, I have to let them know I'm not signing the contract – that's the first thing. And then I need to get my place on the market for sale. It shouldn't be too hard to sell it. It's a pretty modest condo – in an exclusive community, but not some kind of crazy multi-million dollar mansion, you know? And then I have to arrange to move my stuff. Not all of my stuff – I don't think I want the furniture, either. Just my clothes and instruments, and some other things."

"How long will that take?" Alice asked.

"I don't know, but I'll call you and I'll make sure you know what's going on every step of the way." Closing the distance between them, Misty drew Alice into her arms. "I'm not leaving you again, I swear."

With a nod, Alice finally pulled her hands from her pockets and instead slid them into Misty's, curling them around the curve of her backside. "Did I remember to tell you tonight how fantastic you look? What's with the buckling corset?"

"This old thing?" Misty rolled her eyes and shook her head. "Something I kept from a show I did in '98."

"It's pretty sexy." Heat ignited within Alice as she looked at how the corset hugged Misty's slender body, giving the illusion that she was curvy. She wore a black blouse under it, which minimized the appearance of cleavage. Alice liked it. Misty somehow managed to look sexy without flaunting herself or putting a lot of skin on display.

The singer's head dipped toward hers and their lips met in a slow, salty-sweet kiss that left Alice tingling, especially between her legs. With a tug, she drew Misty past the living room, beyond the kitchen, and down the hall. As soon as they entered the bedroom, Alice shut the door with her foot. When the door latched into place, Alice drew her hands from Misty's pockets and up along her back. She loved tracing Misty's lithe frame. When she reached her neck, Alice laced her fingers behind it and tilted her head for another kiss.

Misty let out a low murmur against her mouth and Alice felt her melt against her. Despite the little voice in her head that told her she couldn't be sure Misty would return, Alice went with her feelings, the feelings that were urging her to kiss Misty until neither of them could think clearly.

She turned and guided Misty back toward the bed.

"No, not tonight... Not this time." Misty's fingers

gripped her arms and turned them so Alice was the one backed up against the bed.

"So the corset turns you into badass dominatrix Misty?" Alice joked when she saw the twinkle in her girlfriend's eyes.

"Not quite, but we can always explore that one of these days."

Alice's heartbeat quickened in response to Misty's words. "Promise?" she asked breathlessly.

"I'll be back. Don't doubt that." Misty silenced her with another kiss. Alice clung to her and finally let Misty lay her down on the bed.

Raising herself up on her elbows, Alice watched as Misty undid her jeans and worked them down over her legs. It had been hard to resist putting on a rather racy pair of red panties, just in case Misty did come home with her, and now Alice was glad for the choice. As Misty removed her shirt, Alice wondered what she would think of the almost see-through lace of her matching red bra.

Misty took a step back and inhaled sharply, a sound that sent a chill over Alice's exposed skin. "You like?"

Alice whispered, feeling shy. It was the first time she had tried on seductive underthings in hopes of being seen in them.

"Oh yes, very much. You're more adventurous than I am." Misty reached out and traced the straps of the bra. Her warm fingers felt like they left trails of fire along Alice's skin. When they passed lightly over her nipples, she gasped and arched her back. Misty continued to caress her with barely-there touches that left Alice desperate for more contact.

"You did it to me, so now it's my turn," Misty purred, leaning over her until her lips were within an inch of Alice's, yet just out of reach of an actual kiss.

As Alice's breath hitched with longing, Misty dragged her fingers down along her torso. They skated over her soft stomach, taking a moment to trace the lingering stretch marks – evidence of her pregnancy with Liza.

"You're one of the strongest women I know and I love you for everything you are, everything you've been, and everything you will be."

Alice blinked at Misty's words. "That's…"

"That's how much I love you." Misty kissed her again, her tongue dancing along Alice's. Alice loved how vulnerable she felt, almost naked and lying beneath Misty, who was dictating every move in their lovemaking.

"Take your clothes off," Alice said when Misty stood.

"I don't think so." Those fingers returned to Alice's abdomen, working their way down across her pelvis and then sweeping over her panties. Alice lifted her hips eagerly. However, Misty seemed intent on teasing her, on bringing her to the edge, but not letting her fall over it just yet.

The pressure against her body increased just as the throbbing between her thighs did, Misty's hands sweeping more firmly over her pelvis and then down, gliding over her panties, and all the way down to her ankles. Alice squirmed and watched Misty kneel between her legs.

"Let's get these socks off. The least sexy thing anyone can do is wear socks to bed," Misty said, kissing the insides of her knees as she pulled the offending garments off Alice's feet.

"Yes, let's make this a sock-free zone," Alice quipped, trying to push the sensual haze from her mind. It claimed her once again, though, as Misty worked her way back up her legs and finally let her hands rest on Alice's pelvis.

Alice watched as Misty leaned closer and then drew the very tip of her nose up along her pussy lips, which she knew were visible through the panties. The stroke sent a current through her that made her shake with need.

"Good. You want more." Misty's hands pressed on her with more force, holding her in place as she opened her mouth over Alice's opening and let out a long, hot breath that permeated her wispy panties.

The teasing was driving her crazy and Alice wondered how much longer Misty would keep at it, making her wriggle and gasp. Then she felt Misty's fingers curl over the top of her panties and pull them down. Cool air made her exposed, aching wetness feel even more sensitive.

Misty returned to her place between Alice's thighs and this time it was her tongue that explored her flesh, parting it and delving into the wet seam. Alice no longer had the strength to support herself, so she fell back onto the bed, her breasts bouncing as she reached out to grip the blanket. It twisted in her fists and her body tensed under Misty's deep, probing licks.

She felt Misty's hands on her hips, steadying her so Misty could keep lapping at her. That gifted tongue curled as if gathering Alice's dew, collecting it, savoring it. Alice felt her hips shimmy in response. The tension was spreading from her core, filling her body, winding tighter and tighter.

"Don't stop." The demand was breathless, barely audible. "Please, Misty, I want to come."

She wasn't sure if Misty heard her, but Alice heard the soft, wet sounds of Misty licking and sucking at her pussy. Then she felt the pressure of that strong, searching tongue against her clit. That was all it took to elicit the orgasm from Alice, to send her body into uncontrollable quivering, her hips jolting to meet Misty's mouth.

It seemed to go on forever. Alice felt like she was soaring with bliss, her body folding in on itself just to continue to rub her sensitive clit against Misty's tongue. If she was loud in her pleasure, she didn't care. It was too overwhelming and beautiful for her to worry about who heard her.

And then her body relaxed, still twitching, but no longer riding the wave of ecstasy. Misty pressed a kiss against her inner thigh as Alice collapsed back against the bed. She felt delirious with pleasure and it took several minutes to catch her breath.

But at long last, she did and found that Misty had undressed and was lying next to her, looking into her eyes.

"That was…" Alice took a breath. "Incredible. Really."

"I know." Her girlfriend looked very pleased with herself as she reached for Alice's wrist and said, "I want you to know how I felt, doing that to you." She guided Alice's hand between her legs and reclined on the pillows, so she could splay them open for her.

"Oh my." Pushing herself up on her other arm, Alice explored Misty's slit with her fingers. It was juicy with desire and Alice slid two fingers inside of Misty. She was rewarded with a gasp as she scooted closer to Misty, to press their bodies together.

With her fingers well-occupied, Alice dropped her head to Misty's beautiful, round breasts. She did not waste her time closing her lips over one of her nipples and drawing it deep into her mouth as her hand worked between Misty's open legs.

"Yes, just like that." Misty fell back against the pillow with a groan and offered her body to Alice.

Each rub of Alice's hand against Misty's velvety flesh drew another moan from her. The way she shuddered and vibrated under Alice made her even more determined to please Misty, to give her the same ecstasy she had just experienced. So she worked her fingers even deeper, adding another to fill Misty completely. As she continued to kiss and lick at those pink, budded nipples, she pressed her thumb against Misty's straining clitoris.

Her reward was Misty's trembling increasing in intensity, her entire body shaking as it gathered itself in ever-tightening tension. And then Misty's hips spasmed almost hypnotically, up and down, gyrating against Alice's firm hand as she orgasmed.

"Oh my... my... holy..." Misty's arms clasped around Alice's shoulders, holding her in a tight embrace. "I love you so much," she said in a rush.

Alice raised her head and looked down into Misty's eyes, eyes that were hazy with ecstasy. "I love you too," she answered.

"Good." Her girlfriend drew her even closer, clamping one leg over Alice's and tightening her embrace. "I'm so glad we figured that out." Over time, her breathing evened. As she fell asleep, Misty's grip on Alice slackened slightly, so Alice was able to free herself, reach down, and draw the covers over the two of them.

As they lay in bed curled up against each other, Misty looking radiant and tranquil in sleep, Alice wished the night would never end, but she knew it had to.

Soon.

Chapter 16

Misty glared at the piece of paper Rick slid in front of her. "Really? You expect me to sign this?"

"Of course I do." Rick waved the pen in the air, looking a bit like a bleach blond maniac. "By signing on for another ten years, they've got your back. What are you waiting for?"

What a stupid question. Misty could think of a list of several things she was waiting for, and professional slavery was not one of them. No. At the top of the list was going home to her father and Alice. The second thing was her freedom, which she had since her contract had lapsed. Or would have if the label would stop pestering her and if she could muster the courage to fire Rick as her manager. The problem was she had to do the latter before the former would happen.

"Rick, I can't sign this. There's just no way. It's gone. I'm done with everything." She shook her head. "I just can't make music under their control anymore."

"Oh, please, like that matters. We'll get some European emo to write the songs. All you have to do is sing and play them."

Misty pressed her fingers to her forehead in what she knew was an imitation of one of Alice's gestures. It was funny, she thought, how spending time with people rubbed off on others. Maybe, just maybe, some of Alice's confidence had rubbed off on her, too. "Hey, I've got an idea. Let's go get some lunch in that quiet little place over on Sunset," she said, looking up at him and trying to hold his gaze.

"That hole-in-the-wall dive bar? No thanks."

Misty sat back in her chair and folded her arms. She hated that she had let him into her home today, but she thought meeting on her turf would give her the advantage, would encourage her to cut the cord. Apparently not. She had never been good at ending things. When she did, it always seemed abrupt and brutal, like when she left Alice.

She knew she had to learn to do better than that – to find a way beyond the fear and make a break that she felt good about.

"Oh no…" Rick sat back as well and his eyes narrowed. "You're firing me. I can tell. I've seen this before. Why would you do this? You know no manager will be as dedicated to you as I am. For almost twenty years now, I have labored and sweated and devoted myself to you, and look how far you've come. You're a huge superstar! Yet you choose to do charity gigs, like playing your hometown high school? You are so much bigger than that."

Misty pushed herself out of the chair and crossed the room to look out the huge picture window. Her condo was too spacious for her taste, to pristine, too sterile with its white walls and the white furniture that came with it. But it had been a bargain compared to so many of the other places in L.A. and it was far enough from the hustle and bustle of the city that she could enjoy some peace.

"I don't want to be 'big'," she told Rick. "And I don't want to sing someone else's songs. I want to be free to play the music I want to play, to sing the songs I want to sing. That will never happen under label control."

When she turned back to him, Rick's nose was wrinkled as if he smelled something bad. "You want to be an *artist*," he said distastefully.

"Yeah, I do, and I think I've earned that over the years."

"No, no, no." Rick held his finger up and wagged it. "You were an artist when I picked you up in the 90s, but I turned you into a mega-star. What you've earned is the fame that comes with that – Rock and Roll Hall of Fame level fame. A legacy."

Misty pressed her fingers to her forehead. "Do we really have to fight about this? It's simple – I'm done. I can't do this anymore."

"You can and you should. I thought you loved your life!" Rick also rose from his chair and approached her. "This is what you wanted. It's what you always dreamed of."

"No." Misty raised her gaze to his and shook her head. "The dream I had wasn't to be some kind of superstar. I'm not any of the popular stars today and I don't want to be. There are so many amazing women doing their thing, but I'm not in their league and I don't want to keep pushing myself at this pace. It's too much for me. What I want is to take it back in time to something that means something to me and my fans."

The sigh that huffed from Rick was long and heavy. "Misty," he said, putting his hand on her shoulder, "You can't do that. It's not like you can wake up and have it be the 90s again. Lilith Fair and all that alt stuff is done. It's gone."

"Yeah, well, then I've been doing this too long, if that's how you and the music industry feel." Misty shrugged his hand off her shoulder and waved him away. "I know what I want and I know it's not what the label will want."

"You don't know that. You can't read their minds."

"You're right, but –"

"Great, that settles it." Rick clapped his hands loudly, interrupting Misty. "I'll set a meeting with the execs and we'll go from there. I'm sure we can come to an agreement that makes everyone happy."

"No, Rick, we can't."

"One chance." He backed toward the door, holding his index finger up as he retreated. "One chance, Misty Morse, and we'll make you not just a mega-star, but a happy mega-star."

After he retreated out the door, closing it behind him, Misty turned back to the window and folded her arms. Why couldn't she master the art of breaking up? This was ridiculous. She was a thirty-eight-year-old woman. Why was she letting Rick try to talk her back into this?

She turned and looked around the condo again. It was nice and she did appreciate the fine things in it – the top of the line appliances in the kitchen that were immaculate due to lack of use. The minimalist furniture she never sat on, except when she had rare company, like a visit from a journalist or the label.

Misty wandered into her bedroom. This was one of the two rooms where things happened. Not much, of course. She'd never had a woman in here. It was usually just her, stretched out on the bed, watching television or flipping through a magazine. This was her quiet space. The bathroom attached to it was quite nice, of course, with a large Jacuzzi tub she enjoyed taking long soaks in. But, after almost two weeks in her hometown, as well as spending time with Alice and Liza, her condo was too quiet now. What she wouldn't give for the murmur of the television and the smell of a home cooked meal at this very moment...

With a shake of her head, Misty turned and walked to the other bedroom. This was set up as her own personal office and studio. She had a few precious guitars in here, from the beat-up one she had dragged from Calais to Seattle with her, to the vintage Fender Competition Blue Mustang she had splurged on as a way to celebrate her first gold record. The room was painted a soothing sage green, a corkboard on one wall covered with her favorite photos of her family and friends, and artwork she loved covering the other walls. Her computer sat on a small desk, relatively unused since her cell phone was pretty much her connection to everything. Unlike so many superstars today, Misty only used social media sparingly. She figured the last time she posted to her Twitter account was October... Maybe even the summer time.

Ignoring her computer, which she was sure was gathering an unhealthy amount of dust, Misty sat on her stool and picked up her old guitar. It wasn't the one she traveled with or played in concert anymore, but when her fingers closed around the neck, it felt like embracing an old friend.

She settled it across her lap and dragged her fingers lightly down the strings. The sound wasn't as high quality as her newer instruments, but it brought her back. Back to garage band days and brilliant red maple leaves, to lyrics jotted in a shaky hand on lined notebook paper, while her best friend sat beneath the tree, knees drawn up with a book resting against them.

"Don't go breakin' my heart," Alice would sing in a wavering, untrained voice.

"I couldn't if I tried," Misty would sing back.

"You should market that shit."

"I couldn't if I tried," would be the repeated lyric.

Misty knew even then that she was in love with Alice and she hoped Alice was in love with her. But she never pursued it, because what if – there was the fear, raising its ugly head again – what if Alice rejected her? And then instead of a friendship, instead of never leaving each other's sides, Alice might avoid her completely.

By the time Alice made her feelings completely clear, Misty had already laid out an escape plan. Go to

Seattle, focus on her music, not spend her life torturing herself, wondering whether or not her love was requited or, worse, grow to resent Alice because she was unsure of their love. Or resent her because one little critique of her music.

She took a deep breath and strummed the guitar again.

It was the biggest mistake of her life, a life she had based on all the "what ifs."

It was in the past now, thanks to her loving, understanding girlfriend. She wanted all of those mistakes to be in the past. She wanted her fearful "what ifs" to be a thing of the past, too.

But she never wanted to forget any of it entirely.

So she wrote a song about it.

***

Misty set her old guitar aside and wandered into the kitchen. Her cell phone sat on the counter, vibrating every few seconds. She picked it up and tapped the message notification. There it was – the text from Rick saying, *Weds 8 a.m. with the execs. Be there.*

The phone felt heavy in her hand and it finally tipped

from her loosening fingers to clatter to its original place on the counter. It was Monday evening, almost supper time here in L.A. That meant it was later in Vermont. Going on nine in the evening. The darkness beyond her windows made it feel so much later than even that.

Misty frowned at the phone and went to open her fridge. Of course it was empty. She had been gone for over a week. Turning back to the cell phone, she picked it up and swiped through her contacts until she found her favorite Indian restaurant. Once she had placed her order for delivery, she looked at the "Call Ended" screen for long moments.

She had just over twenty-four hours to fret about the Wednesday meeting. How would she put her foot down in there, surrounded by Rick and the execs, all pressuring her to sign the contract? They were going to put the heat on, because the existing contract had expired three days ago.

It was so much easier for Alice. There was something about her that was confident, always sure of herself. That kind of self-assurance came naturally to Alice, but not to Misty, and she gripped the phone wondering if she could ever figure out how to channel it for herself. Some people seemed to think it was as easy as just making the decision to say or do something, but Misty knew she would feel outnumbered in that meeting.

She couldn't do it alone.

She thumbed her way to her text message screen and reached out to the one person she thought could help her.

I can't do this without you.

Chapter 17

At least I didn't have to drive her to the airport.

Alice rested her chin on her hand and stared down at
the plate of food in front of her. It wasn't often that she
lost her appetite, but it seemed when she did, Misty was
the reason. Only a week ago, she hadn't been able to eat
because she dreaded seeing and talking to Misty. Now
she couldn't eat, because she missed her so much, her
heart ached.

Just when they'd recaptured their friendship and
taken the next step…

"Hey, are you going to be all right?" Deb waved a
hand in front of her face.

"I don't think she's going to make it," Derek
answered, his voice sounding far away.

I didn't have to drive her to the airport, but that
doesn't make it any easier. We waited so long to be
together, I don't think I can do this.

Alice blew out a long breath and poked at the
hamburger. It was still hot, but the idea of eating it made
her queasy.

"Well, shit. Somebody needs to pull her out of this."

"No, Deb, nobody needs to pull me out of this."
Alice looked up at her friends and shrugged. "Look, I'm
loving this whole Monday night idea to ease us back into
the work week and out of the holiday fun, but…" She
shook her head.

"But you're exhausted from humping Misty
constantly?" Deb asked.

Derek narrowed his eyes and said, "I feel like I do
not belong in this conversation."

"Of course you do. You're Alice's friend. Make her
feel better." Deb smacked her brother on the arm and he
met Alice's gaze.

Clearing his throat, Derek said, "Well, um,
congratulations on getting a better girlfriend than I ever
could."

Alice half-smiled and Deb squawked, "Look at that!
She doesn't look miserable anymore!"

"No, but I still feel miserable." Alice picked up a
French fry and stared at it. "I'm in love and I don't know
when I'm going to see her again."

Deb leaned across the table, her gaze sympathetic.
"Look, Alice, you can't blame the fries for that. We

know you miss Misty, but she'll be back. She promised. You can't sit here and not eat. She's not going to be happy if you don't take good care of yourself and that awesome kid of yours while she's gone."

"I know that. I'm just… really busy with this whole pining thing. Too busy to eat."

"Alice, we know you better than anyone, except maybe your daughter. Your 'busy' is the usual bullshit with you avoiding thinking about what you feel. Text Misty and tell her how you feel. She'll let you know how much she misses you too, I'm sure." Deb's eyes darted to the phone that lay on the table beside Alice's plate and then back to her face. "Has she contacted you?"

"Other than this morning to let me know when she landed? No."

"Okay, so she's probably busy, then. I mean, if what you told us is true, she's ditching her record label and her manager, and then putting her house up for sale. That's a lot of work. I bet you'll hear from her tonight. Remember, it's only about three in the afternoon out there. She might be doing the stuff she needs to do to move back here, you know? The more you let her get done during the day, the sooner she comes home."

Even though she knew Deb was right, Alice still felt her chest go cold. "I need to use the restroom."

"Fine," Deb said, casting one last glance at the cell phone. "But if you don't come back to the table in five minutes, I'm calling in the National Guard."

After Alice walked into the bathroom, she leaned against the sink and ran some cool water. Cupping her hands, she collected the water to rub over her face. She was re-learning just how unreasonable love was. Together with Misty, everything was blissful, but apart…

She's coming back. She said so herself. She's coming back and the two of us are going to have a life together.

Alice pushed herself away from the sink and turned off the water. Her reflection looked pale and tired, and her mind was seizing on every irrational fear it could, but she knew she had to take Misty at her word this time. They had both grown up, both seen where they went wrong all those years ago. She refused to repeat her mistakes. That meant giving Misty room to work things out on her own and not expecting to be included in every little thing.

But if they were together now – if Alice could call Misty her girlfriend – didn't she have a right to be involved?

Even after she returned to the table and poked at the food on her plate while Deb and Derek tried to talk to her, Alice mulled over the question. She couldn't let it go after finally eating her burger and half the fries. Or after going home and taking a long, hot bath, or while flipping through channels looking for the cheesiest possible infomercials.

Liza tried to cheer her up, but Alice simply waved her off with a, "Go on. Save yourself." Of course, Liza had remained on the couch next to her, trying to make her smile, trying to get her to ingest copious amounts of candy and junk food. It was Liza who finally gave up and trudged back to her room.

By only nine that evening, Alice was ready to go to bed. If only she had taken the rest of the week off, so she could hide away from the world. At least her one consolation was she had to work. It was one way to force her mind to think about other things. Turning off the TV, Alice walked down the hall toward her bedroom.

She shut the door and stared at the bed. The blankets were still rumpled from that morning. Alice hadn't had the heart to smooth them or wash them since the last night Misty had spent there. The sheets still smelled like her – a heady mix of her coconut shampoo and the cinnamon from the cookies they had snuck into bed at one point in the middle of the night.

Alice stared at the sheets and tried to calm her racing heart. *She's coming back. Deb is right. I just have to be patient. She's got twenty years worth of her life to totally rearrange, after all.*

On the bedside table, her cell phone chimed a text notification. Alice approached the table and jabbed at her phone's screen until the message displayed.

I can't do this without you.

Alice stared at it, eyes wide. She read the message three times before her mind kicked into full gear again. "Liza!" she yelled. When there was no response, she flung the door open and knocked on Liza's door.

"What did I do?" Her daughter flung the door open

and glared at her. "You never yell at me."

"This." Alice showed her the text and Liza read it, her eyes scanning the screen.

"That's so sweet, but what does she want?"

"I'm not sure, but I can either ask for clarification or get out there." Alice fumbled and the phone fell out of her hands, hitting the carpet. "Shit!"

Liza bent and scooped it off the floor. "Alright, calm down. It's not broken. We need to get you out there. Do you have her address in L.A.?"

"Yeah."

"Good." Liza held the phone in front of her started swiping her thumbs over it so fast, Alice couldn't keep up. "Alright, you do this. I'll be fine on my own. If you want, I'll see if I can stay at Tori's house until you get back."

"Are you sure?" Alice asked, looking at the screen Liza had brought up for her.

The teenager nodded. "Of course I am. You love her and, well, she said it – she can't do it without you."

"Right." Alice took the phone and pressed it over her heart. "She can't do it without me." A smile curved her lips and she turned to her room, then stopped and looked back at her daughter. "Thanks, kiddo."

Chapter 18

Misty paced around the lobby, her hands clenching and unclenching. It was rare that they made her wait like this. She was an A-lister. Or did not having a contract anymore make her a... non-lister? A shiver ran through her and she tossed her long, dark ponytail.

That's what she wanted to be. Not some recording slave, but her own person.

"Miss Morse?" The receptionist beckoned to her and then pointed toward the hallway. "They'll see you now in the first conference room."

"Thanks." Misty turned to the hallway as the elevator dinged. She whipped her head around to look over her shoulder and then turned back to the hall. It was just some suit disembarking, not the person she hoped to see. Of course, she was hoping for something unlikely and she knew she had to let it go.

Squaring her shoulders, she continued her walk along the hall. The conference room was enclosed in glass and she couldn't let them see her sweat. She lifted her chin and let her gaze shift to the right.

There they were – the execs she had come to see,

along with Rick. There were two of them, both looking very shark-like with their slicked-back hair and black suits, an intimidating counterpoint to Rick's bleached, spiky hair and white suit.

Oh yeah, she was very familiar with Ray and Jamie. They were hardcore when it came to negotiating. Hardcore as in passive-aggressive and manipulative. Misty knew their game. So how the hell was she going to counter it?

She pushed through the glass door as she told herself, *Whatever you do, do it like a boss. What would Joan Jett do?*

"Misty!" Rick trilled in a too-high voice. "I think you're going to be very pleased with what these fine gentlemen have in mind for you in 2017."

"Okay, let's hear it." Misty lowered herself into one of the chairs and leaned back. From the moment she first saw this conference room years ago, she'd wished she had the courage to put her booted feet up on the polished conference room table. But she kept them on the floor and leaned back in her chair, hoping she looked at least somewhat relaxed.

Ray did sit on the table, though. Or, rather, lifted one butt cheek onto it and let his other leg sort of dangle close to the floor. Misty knew he liked that position because it gave him physical height over whomever he was trying to work with – her, producers, managers. Rick was usually the one on the receiving end of that position, since it was up to him to negotiate her contracts, but since she was on the verge of cutting Rick loose, it looked like they were now dealing directly with her.

"Rick shared your concerns with us and they're valid. You're no longer some young ingénue, but you're still a hot commodity, even in your middle age."

Misty bristled, but simply gritted her teeth and nodded. He made it sound like "middle age" was a curse of some kind and like she was livestock.

"So let's look at your image and see if that's the problem. Maybe it's not that you don't want to record with us anymore, but rather that you're ready for a change of how we position you."

You mean not bent over, taking your deal and not complaining about it? Misty swiveled her chair slightly and looked past Ray at the clock.

"I'm sorry, am I boring you?"

Misty turned back to him. She hadn't realized her little maneuver made him feel unimportant. All she wanted to do was not have to look at him sneering down at her. "Maybe just a little bit," she said and winked at him. "Go on, though, if you want and I'll try to stay awake."

It was the first time she had ever thrown that kind of attitude at… anyone, really. And it made her feel pretty powerful. It also made her want to write again, to put her feelings into lyrics and music.

Ray glanced over his shoulder at Jamie, who then looked at Rick. She knew they weren't accustomed to her giving them a hard time, not since her earlier days with the label. After the initial contract, she had fallen into line so easily, thinking she had exactly what she wanted. But every move she'd made was not her own then.

She was ready to make her own moves now.

"So as you're…" Ray cleared his throat.

"…maturing, shall we say? Yes, as you're maturing, it's

obvious you'd have a different look and sound in mind. I mean, how long have you been dyeing your hair that same shade of brown?"

Misty tried not to grimace. "Unlike Rick's little anime do, this is my natural color," she said.

"Sure it is." The exec chuckled and looked at Jamie as if for confirmation. The other suit chimed in with laughter, followed by Rick, who was actually blushing with embarrassment. "So here's what we have in mind for you."

Jamie lifted up a square board with an album cover mock-up. "It's called 'Crisis'," he said.

"Excuse me?" Misty furrowed her brow and looked the cover up and down. "It's just a gray blob over a faded leopard print with the word 'Crisis' splashed across it."

"No, it's the gray of life diminishing our spots as we transition from youth to old age."

"Old age?" Misty squawked. "I know seventy-year-old women who are far from 'diminished,' as you put it."

There went her cool.

With a long breath through her nose, she closed her eyes and whispered, "You're on the wrong track. This isn't going to make my fans happen. It's going to alienate the fuck out of them, just like it's alienating me."

"Are you sure this isn't the way to go?" Ray leaned toward her. "Are we really that out of touch? Come on, Misty. Be real with us. Why else would you decide you didn't need us if it wasn't for a midlife crisis?"

Misty wasn't sure how to react. In that moment, her heart froze and cold radiated through her body. She was sure she was about to hyperventilate. And if she opened her eyes, she thought she might cry. They had insulted not just her, but a huge demographic of people.

And she knew what they were doing. They were trying to make her feel disempowered and small. Well, it was working.

She heard something bang and then slam, and a familiar voice said, "Am I too late for the meeting?"

Alice!

When Misty's eyes flew open, she saw Alice standing just inside the door, legs braced apart and hands on her hips. She looked like her usual feisty self, a body hugging teal blue dress wrapped around her and heels that made her at least two inches taller. Was this woman middle aged? Yes. Diminished? Absolutely not.

"Sorry about that. The air traffic was ridiculous." Alice batted her eyelashes and strolled over to stand behind Misty's chair. "Got here as quick as I could, though, so carry on." Herwarm hands settled on Misty's shoulders and squeezed them reassuringly.

"I'm sorry, and you are…?"

"Oh, I'm Misty's biographer. She asked me to keep up with her every move, document her life, you know? It's going to make a fascinating book and a big, fat royalty check, if you know what I mean." Alice's hands tightened over Misty's shoulders and Misty bit back a laugh.

"Fine, write whatever the fuck you want. Just shut up and let us proceed." Ray looked back down at Misty.

The cold deep within Misty thawed. How dare he talk to Alice like that? No one in their right mind would tell Alice to stay quiet. Not feisty Alice. She would bark like a dog and bite his head off, and he would be sorry he ever said anything to her.

Except it was Misty who rose from the chair and barked, "That'll be enough of your bullshit, Ray." She pointed at the album cover. "That is insulting as fuck, not just to me, but to all women. Shove it up your ass, Jamie. There's nothing left – that contract expired and I won't be signing a new one. Ever. Rick, you're fired. I'm going off to make some real fucking art, now. Come on, Alice."

Misty turned to the door and yanked it open. She didn't bother to look behind her to see if Alice was following. She knew by the purposeful clacking of the heels that her girlfriend was right there, striding along behind her.

She even heard Alice blow a kiss to the receptionist and say, "See? I didn't crash the party too hard."

As soon as the two of them were in the elevator together, Misty turned and gathered Alice in her arms. Their lips met in a crushing kiss, Alice's arms twining behind Misty's neck to hold her close. The doors opened and they stepped out of the elevator, hand in hand, walked through the office building doors, and out into the warm L.A. sunshine.

Chapter 19

"I can't believe you did this." Misty pointed her spoon at Alice and shook her head. "I can't believe you're here."

Alice grinned. She couldn't believe it either, but she was glad. As she dug into her ice cream, she said, "Well, when I got your message, I jumped on the first flight I could get to LAX. You said you couldn't do it without me and I wasn't about to make you go it alone."

"Thank you for that."

"I also have some good news for you. That place you were scouting as a possible studio is still available and I told the landlord to hold it for you."

"You did?" Misty stared at her. "When did you do that?"

"Yesterday when I was waiting to board the flight." Alice put the spoonful of chocolate ice cream in her mouth and savored it. "Oh, and Liza cannot wait to help with production of your next album, if you'll let her."

"Um, yes. That would be fantastic."

289

"Great." Looking around the condo, Alice said, "I can see why you don't care about keeping this place. It's just not you."

"It isn't?"

"No. I mean, your room back home was always more creative than this. You had those stars on the ceiling and dark curtains – not this perfect white crap." Alice gathered another spoonful of ice cream. "Really, Misty, you need to come home. You belong at home."

As Alice watched, Misty ducked her head and flushed slightly. "Yeah, I figured that out when I was there, even before you and I made up."

"So, after we finish celebrating your freedom, are you going to give me a tour of your place?" Alice played with the ice cream in her dish. It was partially melted, just the way she loved it.

"Of course. Uh…" Misty used her spoon to point. "This is the kitchen, where we're sitting. There's the living room. Very open floor plan. And then there's two bedrooms. I use one as an office and then the other for sleeping."

"How do you get by without a bathroom?" Alice

asked.

"It's a struggle, believe me."

Alice laughed and stirred her ice cream. Everyone had been right – she and Misty would be together again. When she laughed again, Misty kicked her under the table.

"What's so funny?"

Looking up at her, Alice couldn't help but smile at the expression on her face. "I'm your knight in shining armor," she said. "You needed rescuing from your own dream."

"You're the tiniest knight I've ever seen."

"Yes, but I'm that much more effective, because people will underestimate me."

Misty scoffed and shook her head. "I think at this point, I've lived out that first dream. It was grand while it lasted, but my dream changed. I just know I want to be back home with you."

"Funny how life works." Curling her fingers around her bowl, Alice traced them through the condensation. "My dream has never changed. I always wanted to be a librarian and a genealogist, and I always wanted to do those things with you at my side."

"Maybe that's where I went wrong – I left you out. Maybe this whole thing would have been better if I had just stuck with the original plan." Misty bowed her head.

"No, that's not necessarily true." Alice laid her hand over Misty's wrist. Her girlfriend's skin felt too hot to the touch. "Don't beat yourself up. We moved past that, remember? I didn't do a good job of making my point, which was supposed to be that we're all different. For some people, it's like they have a road map from birth. I'm one of those people who always knew I would do XYZ. You're not and it's okay for your dream to change. I bet even if I was here with you all along, it would have changed and, knowing you, you wouldn't have admitted to it, because you would have been concerned about my happiness or something. It would have taken you this long to figure it out and decide you were done."

Misty put her hand over Alice's. "You always knew me better than anyone else, so I still have to admit it was a mistake to do all of this without you."

Alice waved her off. "Stop it." She stood and leaned

over the table to kiss Misty, her lips slanting down over hers. "Stop it," she said again. When she saw the way Misty was watching her, butterflies fluttered in her stomach. "Stop it," she whispered, framing Misty's face with her hands and giving her another kiss.

There was the sound of chair legs along the floor and then Misty was on her feet. They both angled their bodies around the table and Alice felt her breath whoosh from her body as Misty pulled her into her arms. There was no more delicious feeling for Alice than her curves molding to Misty's as they stumbled toward the bedroom together.

The air wafted across her skin as Misty removed her wrap dress easily, leaving her in her panties and bra. Alice lost her breath again as Misty pressed her back against a wall, still kissing her, leaving her dizzy with need.

When they parted, Misty was wearing a mischievous half-smile. "This is the most action this bedroom has ever seen."

"Oh, isn't that delightful?" Alice wriggled, loving the feel of Misty's hands on either side of her torso. "I feel very special. I can't wait to pop your bed's cherry."

"Let's start here first. The bed is just one of many options."

As Alice watched, Misty lowered herself to kneel before her, peeling the panties down over Alice's hips. Misty's lips pressed against Alice's slick petals and she gasped. Her stance widened and she leaned back against the wall, the only thing keeping her upright as Misty's tongue delved into her. Alice watched as Misty pleasured her, lapping at her pussy, her gaze intent on Alice's face.

It was certainly the most erotic experience of Alice's life to watch Misty watching her. She knew there were myriad expressions flickering across her face in response to the bliss coursing through her. Alice gave in to the desire to reach down and tangle her hands in Misty's hair, threading her hands through the smooth strands, loosening the ponytail just enough to hold her in place between her legs.

Alice gave in to the moment. It wasn't as though she could control her body anyway, as her hips gyrated back and forth sensually along Misty's searching, tasting tongue. Every time it slipped over her clit, she let out a cry of ecstasy. Before she knew it, her entire body was tightening, tensing until she didn't think she could stand it anymore. And then the tension shattered, filling her with electric fire that radiated throughout her. She saw starbursts behind her closed eyelids and felt her legs give way.

When Alice sagged away from the wall, Misty rose and wrapped her arms around her waist. "I've got you," she whispered.

"Yes." Alice leaned against her and sought a kiss, tasting herself on Misty's lips and tongue.

Misty turned her to the bed and Alice bent over it, stretching as she recovered. Misty chuckled and rubbed her hand in warm circles on her exposed bottom. "Is this an invitation?" she asked.

"Do you want it to be?" Alice looked over her shoulder and winked. "I didn't really bring anything to use in that area, but maybe you have a secret stash of toys we could play with."

When Misty blushed, Alice let out a soft giggle. "Really? Oh, you have got to tell me where they are, so I can make you feel as good as you made me feel."

"No, forget it. Let's just snuggle up."

"It's barely lunchtime. No snuggling." Alice reached for the bedside table and opened the drawer. "Ah ha!" Inside she saw only one item – a slightly curved white vibrator. She picked it up and switched it on.

Misty looked at her with a funny expression on her face. "I've never used that with another person."

"So now you're going to." Alice crawled to the edge of the bed and beckoned to her. "It's going to be so much fun," she purred, rising up on her knees and kissing Misty's neck.

With slow movements, Misty removed her shirt and pants, but she stood at the edge of the bed, still watching.

"Trust me, I'll be gentle." Alice took her by the hand and coaxed her onto the bed. "I just want to play with you. We should enjoy ourselves. It's just you and I in this place, no one to bother us, no place to be. You've got me until tomorrow, so let's make the most of it."

"Just until tomorrow?" The pout on Misty's face was so endearing, Alice couldn't help but kiss those full lips.

"Yes," she said. "But you'll be with me before you

know it. Now, let's have just a little more fun together until then." Alice ran her hand lightly over Misty's shoulders and down to her breasts as she slid the vibrator between her legs.

Misty trembled beneath her touch and murmured, "I better lie down."

"Yes, you better." Alice followed her movements, keeping the vibrator against her as Misty sank down against the pillows. "It occurs to me that we need to buy another one, since I don't have one for myself. You'll have to let me know how this works out for you and if you recommend it."

With a smirk, Alice hooked her finger in Misty's panties and moved the fabric aside, so the vibrator could find its mark – her girlfriend's delicate bud of pleasure. Misty's legs fell wide as Alice stroked the vibrator slowly across her skin, then pressed it firmly in place.

"Those things... work... fast," Misty said, her breathing becoming hectic and her hips starting to buck.

"Really?" Alice watched Misty's reaction – how her entire body relaxed against the pillows, while her hips moved back and forth, demanding more stimulation, more ecstasy. Alice kept the vibrator pressed against her just a moment longer, before removing it and leaning forward to suck at her clit. That seemed to take the edge off, as Misty's body settled down against the bed, so Alice applied the humming toy to her again, circling it over her sensitive flesh.

Each breath that passed Misty's lips seemed sharper than the last, more frantic. Her body rose up to meet the vibration and she squeezed her eyes shut as her entire body quivered with release. Alice circled the vibrator even more firmly over Misty's clit, drawing out her reaction as long as she possibly could, until her girlfriend pushed her away with a moaned, "No more..."

Alice turned the toy off and set it aside. With a small grin, she slinked between Misty's legs and lay atop her, their breasts meeting softly. "Now I bet you feel incredibly relaxed," she whispered, nestling against her. The scent of Misty's coconut shampoo filled her senses and Alice enjoyed just being there with her, their bodies loosely entwined and sated.

"I don't think I could possibly feel better than this," Misty answered with a low sigh.

"Oh, I bet that's not true."

"You think?"

"Mm." Alice nodded against Misty's neck. "I have plans for you, sweetie. Plans that are going to make you feel wonderful."

Chapter 20

The building wasn't anything special. It stood between a boutique and a photographer's studio in Montpelier. It looked like any other storefront with white siding and a large window, but this window was covered by a darkening blind and black curtains.

When Misty opened the door and walked inside, it didn't matter that it looked like an empty storefront from the outside. Because on the inside, it was hers, purchased outright and renovated with soundproofing.

Liza was already there, along with an older man who was nodding along as she made changes to the controls on the digital audio workstation. Whatever she was mixing sounded good and the man at her side gave his approval.

"You have a great ear, Liza. I think she's going to be pleased when she hears this."

"Hears what?" Misty asked.

Liza turned and smiled. "Hey, Misty. Gregory was just showing me how to mix tracks. This is a way better set-up than the one I have on my computer at home. So pro!"

"That's the idea. I'm glad you two are getting to know each other. You're learning from the best." Misty removed her coat and hung it on the rack by the door. The enclosed recording studio was beckoning to her with its warm light and deep orange painted walls. So far she had done half a dozen songs since returning to Vermont. Spring was nearly here and she hoped to have an independent album to drop by the first day of fall, if not sooner.

The door opened again and Alice walked in, a full drink carrier in her hands. "Coffee, anyone?" She set it on the bare desk by the front door. They didn't need a receptionist just yet – just a place to set random stuff when the studio was in use. If Misty ever got to the point where she was recording other artists, the need for office personnel might change.

For now, though, Gregory was her producer, Liza was his apprentice, Alice was the purveyor of coffee and snacks, and Misty was the talent.

Even though she had been recording for nearly two decades, she still got excited about walking into the booth. She picked up her coffee for a sip before sliding into the booth, shutting the door behind her, putting the headphones over her ears, and stepping up to the mic.

Alice sat on the other side of Gregory at the workstation, grinning from ear to ear. This was the way they spent their Saturdays since late January. Gregory had produced Misty's first album "way back when," before going back east to focus on indie singers. She was glad she had stayed connected to him and managed to get him in her corner on this project.

"Today's an exciting one," Misty said into the mic. When she saw blank faces looking back at her from the other side of the glass, she tapped the mic and said, "Um, is this thing hot or what?"

She saw Gregory nudge Liza, who scrambled to press a button and then move a series of levers to modulate the sound. Liza gave her a thumbs-up and Misty tried again.

"Can you hear me now?"

"It depends," Alice answered, leaning up to the intercom that transmitted her voice into the recording booth. "Are you trying out for a cell phone commercial?"

"Very cute. Let's do this." Misty grinned when Alice blew her a kiss. "I'm so glad I saved this song for today," she said, nodding at Liza.

Liza gave her another thumbs up and cued the music, looking at Gregory for confirmation that she had done it correctly.

The music filled Misty's ears and she closed her eyes, taking a moment to feel the beat and get her mind where she wanted it. Most songs required several takes and she knew this would be no different. But she loved the idea of nailing it the first time, relished the notion of seeing the look on Alice's face when she heard the lyrics.

Opening her mouth, Misty let the words tumble out, layering them over the melody. Each line brought her deeper into the song and she swayed to the music. It was as close to dancing as she ever got, but it was how she expressed her feelings physically.

Misty didn't keep her eyes closed in performances, of course, but laying down those first tracks in the studio was different. She wanted to connect only with the words and the music, and that was what she did over the next few minutes as the song built.

At last she was done. It felt like she had lost herself in the music for far longer than the three minutes and forty-seven seconds it took to actually sing the song. Her eyes fluttered open and she saw Liza glowing with excitement, Gregory tapping some controls and nodding with approval, and Alice…

Alice was gaping at her, eyes soft with adoration as she looked at Misty. She mouthed "Holy shit" and her expression shifted to an even gentler one, full of love.

"I think we got it," Gregory said, finally looking up. His entire focus was on the sound – the recording, the audio levels, the balance between the music and the singing. Misty was thankful that she had been able to work with him again. Few people were as in touch with the "old her," musically-speaking, as he was. He was just the person to bridge the divide between Misty's 1996 sound and what she wanted to create in 2017.

She set the headphones aside and stepped out of the booth. "It's not going to be technically perfect," she said, "but it just felt good getting that first try out of me. What did you think?" Her gaze settled on Alice, who still looked awed by what she had just heard.

Alice leapt from her chair, wrapping her arms around Misty's shoulders and squealing. "I can't believe you wrote a song for me!"

A full-throated laugh emerged from Misty and she hugged Alice tight. "You're my everything. Of course I wrote a song for you. You inspired me to become the person I am and you brought me back to where I want to be. That means a lot to me."

"So what's the name of the album going to be, then? It is also called 'Alice'?"

"No, but I'm not telling until we have the artwork."

Liza opened her mouth. "It's gonna be..."

Misty glared at her and shook her head.

"...the best album ever," Liza finished with a wink. "Seriously, mom, it'll be worth waiting to find out the title track and everything."

"Well, darn it. What are we supposed to do until then?" Alice looked up at Misty.

Affection filled her as she looked back at the woman in her arms. What were they supposed to do until then?

"Just love each other," Misty answered, before brushing her lips over Alice's in a sweet kiss that sent her heartbeat into overdrive.

Epilogue

Catharsis dropped on September 22, the first day of fall and a week before the wedding. Alice turned the CD case around and around in her hands, sighing and grinning like an idiot. Besides the fact that her song was on it, her name was prominently scrawled across the liner notes, printed in an iridescent silvery color that flashed in the light.

It wasn't just the one song, but an entire album dedicated to her by Misty.

"It's like a musical history of our journey," Misty had described it in an interview with a local journalist. "From start to, well, where we are now."

Alice set the CD on her desk, next to the bridal magazine she could probably recycle by now. After all, everything was set – the venue, the dresses, the rings, the flowers… But she loved that reminder that she had spent almost all spring and summer planning a wedding. Picking up the dog-eared magazine, she hugged it to her chest.

In only a week, she and Misty would be married and then they could take a break before Misty started a local college tour, performing songs off her new album. Meanwhile, Alice had a family tree to finish – hers and Misty's, joined at last.

She turned on her heel and walked out of the office. It wasn't exactly her office anymore, since she shared it with Misty now, but that suited her just fine. So did the small changes around the house, like a guitar here and a leather jacket there.

The best part was seeing Misty on the sofa next to Liza, both flinging popcorn at the television screen and giggling.

"I thought we agreed to wait on our *Rocky Horror* night until October," Alice said, glaring at the kernels of popcorn all over the living room carpet.

"No, mom, Misty has pre-wedding jitters. You have to let her relax." Even though Liza's voice was pleading, she didn't look at all contrite or serious.

Misty confirmed Alice's suspicion when she said, "Don't listen to her. I don't have jitters. She just wanted an excuse to throw food."

"I have a feeling Misty's telling the truth." Alice knelt and started gathering the popcorn off the floor.

"Honestly, it's like having two kids, instead of one."

"Yeah, but you love it." Misty lowered herself to the floor to lend a hand.

It was true. Alice did love it. There was nothing better than feeling like her family was complete now that Misty was becoming part of it. With a mock glare, she flung her handful of popcorn at Misty. "You're a terrible influence on Liza."

"No, she's a terrible influence on me."

"And life comes around full circle," Alice said, leaning in to kiss her fiancée.

Titles by the Author

Something About You

Must Love Chickens

Meant to Be

Game of Hearts

All For Love

A Vote for Love

Series

A Charmed Life: The Ashland Witches, Book 1

A Garden Dream: The Ashland Witches, Book 2

A Magick Dance: The Ashland Witches, Book 3

(coming fall 2017)

About the Author

Jea Hawkins writes sweet and spicy contemporary lesbian romance. If love conquers all, then she'd like to think her heroines can rule the world one day. An east coast transplant to the Midwest, she loves to write about complicated women and settings that feel like home.

Personal addictions include autumn, cozy sweaters, hot chocolate, and the Sims 3. She's both an avid reader and gamer, and hopes readers don't mind a few geeky references here and there in her work.

You can keep up with her latest releases by signing up for her newsletter at http://eepurl.com/cVU-pz or by visiting her online at jeahawkins.com.

Printed in Great Britain
by Amazon

33641720R00175